Fic YA Bechka, P.A. 20670
western Hawk's Indians

Galien Township Library
Galien, Michigan

1. Books may be kept two weeks and may be renewed once for the same period, except 7 day books and magazines.

2. A fine is charged for each day a book is not returned according to the above rule. No book will be issued to any person incurring such a fine until it has been paid.

3. All injuries to books beyond reasonable wear and all losses shall be made good to the satisfaction of the Librarian.

4. Each borrower is held responsible for all books charged on his card and for all fines accruing on the same.

Hawke's Indians

Hawke's Indians

P. A. BECHKO

DOUBLEDAY & COMPANY, INC.

GARDEN CITY, NEW YORK

1979

All the characters in this book are fictitious,
and any resemblance to actual persons,
living or dead, is purely coincidental.

Library of Congress Cataloging in Publication Data

Bechko, P A
Hawke's Indians.

I. Title.
PZ4.B39Haw [PS3552.E24]   813'.5'4
ISBN: 0-385-14963-8
Library of Congress Catalog Card Number 78–22610

Hawke's Indians

CHAPTER 1

The train was still several miles down the track, approaching at a brisk, rhythmic pace. As yet Salvador Hawke had not seen it, but he had heard it. The vibration in the rails could be read as plain as a telegraph. Straightening, Hawke brushed the clinging dust from his black pants and once again went to sit before the lopsided old train shack adjacent to the water tank where the train would be pulling in to a stop. Just in case the engineer got other ideas at the last minute, though, he had carefully planted a couple of charges of dynamite on either side of the tracks. The fuses, long ones, led up from the tracks to lay beside the rickety chair where Hawke leisurely awaited the train's appearance.

He puffed slowly on a cigar, something he rarely did, with an air of casual nonchalance that barely concealed the effort it took to keep from erupting into a fit of coughing. Cigars had never set well with him, and Hawke avoided lighting one most of the time, preferring to hold it clenched in his jaws in times of extreme stress. At the moment, though, he needed a spark handy, and the cigar had seemed the easiest way to supply one.

Still in the distance, but drawing steadily nearer, the labored chug-chug of the approaching engine reached Hawke's ears. The terrain here was exceptionally steep in many places, that being the reason for the additional water stop almost in the middle of nowhere. It took a lot of wood and water to keep an engine climbing in the mountains. A faint smile flickered across his face, curving thin lips and bringing a light to narrow blue eyes that usually harbored an inward, reflective expression. A thick black mustache quirked and flared around the root of the smoking cigar, accenting a square face and firm jaw. Curly black hair crept from beneath the black, flat-crowned, broad-brimmed hat

that shaded his eyes from the brilliant afternoon sun. Hawke
continued to smile faintly as he thought about the plug that had
been pulled on the water-storage tank. That would slow them
down considerably. That, combined with the inhospitable country that this just naturally was.

Salvador Hawke had a long-standing dislike for railroads. In
this year of 1903 they were hailed as the transportation of the
future, and they had supposedly improved while spreading their
sphere of influence since their beginnings. That last part Hawke
could readily agree with. Since the arrival of the Atchison,
Topeka, and Santa Fe back in '78 things had done nothing but
change, and as far as Hawke could see, it had been a downhill
slide all the way. Trains were loud, dirty, and, with ravenous
hunger for wood in the tender, could almost devour a forest
while passing through it. In the light of the fact that rails had
been laid right through the middle of the house where he had
been born, Hawke could not think of one redeeming feature possessed by trains.

Hawke glanced up to see the engine puffing around a still-dis-
tant curve. Well, he conceded to himself, there was one redeeming feature. Railroads had provided him with a profession, albeit
one with considerably changing fortunes. Shifting in his seat, he
cocked his head enough to be able to see out from beneath the
broad brim of his black hat. A couple of his men were on that
train, and this time, at least, things should go smoothly. It
should not be difficult to relieve the train of the strongbox it was
hauling for the railroad's own payroll.

It was not as if what they were going to do had not been done
before, by themselves as well as many others, but Hawke was
uneasy and wondered whether he should have been one of the
men on the train. He and the men with him had been at this
game for over nine years now, but lately things had not been
going just right. There was the time up near Denver when the
dynamite charges had not been set right and they had not gone
off until the engine had been a couple of miles beyond where
they had lain in wait. A short time after that Pronto had come
up over the back of a tender to take over an engine near Mora,

fell off, and damn near broke his neck. Several other incidents occurred after those, which Hawke did his best to put out of his mind. Of course, part of it had been caused by pure bad luck, but part of it, he was convinced, was that their timing was off. It was those damn detectives the railroad had hired in an effort to put a stop to the epidemic of railroad robberies. Although Salvador Hawke had never seen any of the three men the railroad had put fresh on their payroll, he did know them by reputation. The names of Tom Fisher, Will Barnett, and Sam West bore ominous import, and when a man had an eye out for them, it was difficult to keep his timing in sinc. Then, if that was not enough, the law was cooperating with a U.S. marshal by the name of Liam Cook. The name was not as familiar to Hawke as the others, but he knew the man had been on their trail for some months. Word had come to him. It was plain fact. Cook had been making about as much progress as a tortoise through soft sand, but nonetheless he was there, somewhere.

The train's progress was steady, almost reassuring in its rhythm. Coming down out of the pass through the high mountains, it began a gradual incline that continued well beyond the water tank. It was a broad, gentle slope, and the engine was not laboring, as it had through the pass when Hawke had first heard it.

As the train continued its slow approach, Hawke watched intently. Ringo and George would be getting itchy as they waited concealed behind some brush and the ramshackle shack with the horses. Hawke suppressed a cough and puffed on the cigar to keep it going. Everything changed. The times changed, the railroad engines changed, everything, except maybe people. Like himself and his men. They fit together neatly, like pieces of a puzzle—each a little odd, but fitting well with the others. In view of the detectives and the U.S. marshal, it occurred to him that it might be a good idea for them all to lay low after they pulled this off. They had never done it before, though Hawke had heard of other gangs doing it, holing up in a town or maybe a hidden valley—somewhere where they could not be found, and even if they were, it would take an army to blast them out. When this was taken care of he would put it to the boys. Hart, George, and Ringo Hawke knew to be reasonable when their pockets were filled with cash, but Pronto would be against it no matter what. Pronto was a man who always wanted to be moving, and he had more Robin Hood in his veins than Hawke himself.

It would take some considering. Again Hawke glanced in the direction of the approaching train. He took the cigar from his mouth, looked at the redly glowing tip, then let his hand drop to his side, touching the burning tip to the fuses propped against his chair. With a soft pop and a sizzle, both caught and started to burn. Hawke smiled his satisfaction. It would make quite a bang.

Usually Pronto was the one to take care of the dynamite, but since he was one of the pair riding the train, Ringo was seeing to it. Hawke had a few misgivings where Ringo's dynamiting abilities were concerned, considering it was he who had set the awkwardly delayed charges near Denver. Pronto had taken him in hand since then, carefully tutoring him in the art so there would be no more foul-ups. This was Ringo's first real trial since the Denver incident, and with the luck they had been having in recent days, Hawke would have preferred to have Ringo on the train and Pronto rigging the fuses. But they had all known Ringo was too recognizable a figure. His starkly white hair, gray eyes, and shifty look were too well known to risk recognition, especially alongside Hart Jackson's dark countenance. Half red man and half black, Jackson towered over the rest of them with meaty, squared shoulders, hard, angular face, soulful brown eyes, and an even, brownish complexion that made his roots undiscernible.

Pronto, whose real name was Jean LaRue, a fact very few people living knew, was a man who could fade into almost any crowd and not be noticed. Or, putting on his thick French accent for the ladies, he could easily be the center of attraction. His small, neatly trimmed black beard, along with flashing black eyes, seemed to hold a fascination for the ladies in spite of his small, slender build. His long, black hair he wore smoothed straight back, helmetlike, from a face distinguished by flat angular planes, and held there by a light application of bear grease or whatever was close to hand. One good look at him usually made the observer certain in their assumption that he had to have sprung from Indian parentage, until he opened his mouth.

The tiny fire at the end of each fuse bounced and sizzled its way along its length under Hawke's critical eye. The train came on. If the timing was just right, the dynamite should blow well ahead of the train's arrival. Hawke got rid of the offending cigar and started to climb to his feet as an uproar erupted behind the shack at his back. A few muttered oaths rode the still mountain air, a horse whinnied, and Hawke was almost certain he heard a snarl.

"What the hell's going on back there?" he demanded, trying not to change his casual stance as the train approached within hailing distance.

"Damn mutt!" Ringo muttered harshly, his voice sounding oddly hollow echoing through the listing shack. "Mutt wandered up from somewheres and Rawlins started to messin' with it. . . ."

"Get rid of it." Hawke cut him off sharply, nearly having to yell above the racket of the train's approach as the brakes were applied and the cumbersome monster started to slow. George Rawlins always did have him a way with animals, but he could pick the damndest times.

In spite of the engine's close proximity, Hawke was sure he could hear more angry snarls as Ringo continued to mutter sharply, "Can't—damn critter won't turn loose a' me."

"Give it a slap on the rump and send it packing!" Hawke ordered, teeth grit, legs braced against the concussion that would accompany the blast Ringo had set near the tracks. Near enough to throw up a lot of dust and make a big bang, but not close enough to tear up the tracks. Hawke did not want the lives of all those people on his head if the engineer decided not to stop. It was not their fault that they were not bright enough not to have anything to do with the railroads in any capacity. Not every man was as determined as Salvador Hawke.

"You ain't seen the size of this here dog," Ringo retorted.

"Rawlins!" Hawke could feel something closely akin to panic beginning to build within him. The dog could be an omen, the beginning, the whole thing could be going sour again. He pushed the possibility from his mind. What the hell was a dog doing out here anyway? "Rawlins, do something about that damn mutt!" he ordered, his voice again steady and ringing with the authority of leadership.

"Sure thing." The lazy drawl was barely audible above the train's grinding to a halt directly in front of Hawke. At almost the same instant the largest terrier-type dog with the most massive square head Hawke had ever seen loped around the side of the old shed, headed directly for the train and the stock cars.

Not until that moment had Hawke realized with a start that the dynamite had not gone off. The engineer waved to him in a friendly gesture, and Hawke glanced uneasily along the length of the fuses until his eye caught the dancing sparks still traveling inexorably toward their destination. Ringo had done it again. The fuses were too long.

"What's goin' on?" Rawlins' voice queried from the rear. "I ain't heard the dynamite yet."

"Shut up!" Hawke muttered out of the side of his mouth. He shifted nervously on his feet. What the engineer thought he might be doing there in the middle of nowhere without a horse was a puzzlement to Hawke, but he hoped the man would not dwell on the matter too thoroughly for the moment.

A couple of stout, swarthy-looking men let down the stock ramps and made ready to unload what appeared to be a couple of cars full of cattle. Hawke remembered the pens he had spotted off to one side, proof that this stop was for more than water, but they had appeared run down, as if they had not been made use of in years. The men unloading the cars appeared to know the strange beast of a dog that sat eagerly waiting at the camp's end, salivating as if he expected to devour each cow as it came down. It was almost enough to send a cold shiver down his spine as his gaze strayed again to the still-burning fuses, then flicked in the direction of the windows lining the side of the passenger car.

There, framed in the glass, Pronto's face peered out at him in questioning disbelief. The touching off of the dynamite was supposed to have been the signal for them all to move. The old engine was starting to take on necessary water from an almost-empty tank, and a man was loading additional tinder on board. Still, nothing had happened.

Hawke tried to appear self-assured, as if all were going as he had planned. Then, abruptly, Pronto's face disappeared from the window. Hawke swore under his breath. Pronto would be taking matters into his own hands. That was how he had gotten his nickname. Everything had to be done fast or he took action of his own. But the problem was that Pronto rarely knew what he was doing. In Pronto's haste, it never occurred to him to think things through before taking action, which was why he was not the leader of their bunch and Salvador Hawke was.

Right now Pronto and Jackson would be heading back for the baggage car, where the strongbox was. Hawke was trying to decide whether that was good or bad when the dynamite blew. The earth shuddered as a crater spewed its center of dust and rock skyward on either side of the tracks. Hawke almost staggered before the force of it, but he managed somehow to keep his footing, muttering under his breath about Ringo's inept handling of the dynamite. The cattle, some of which were already partway down the ramp, did not fare nearly so well. The explosion caused several to stumble to their knees ahead of their fellows, and when they staggered to their feet they were looking for somewhere to run with nowhere to go.

Ringo and Rawlins had broken from cover behind the old railroad shack and were sprinting for the baggage car beneath the startled scrutiny of nearly every passenger on board the train. One face among the many, Hawke noted with his usual eye for detail, was unusually comely. Framed in glossy blue-black hair, her skin was milk white, her lips full and red, and an anxious expression showed in large, catlike brown eyes that stared, for a mere instant, directly at him. Dust and small bits of earth and pebbles were still raining down on Hawke unchecked, as if the sky had somehow opened up and dropped the foul burden, when he touched his hat brim in the curious young lady's direction and bestowed one of his more endearing smiles on her. But Hawke was not aware of the other face a couple of windows down, the eyes also turned in his direction, lighting up with recognition as they spotted him. Neither did Hawke see the owner of the grim face pull back with a jerk to avoid Hawke's gaze and to locate his partner. Will Barnett was on the train with him, and Tom Fisher wished that Sam West was with them there as well. He was to meet them at a stop farther down the line. Sam would be sorry he missed out on the capture. After all, they had been barely put on the case, and now they would be closing it.

The din surrounding the cattle cars was almost deafening as the terrified beasts lunged from one side of the only partially packed car, bellowing their fear and battering themselves against the sides of the cars. It was then that Hawke realized the reason for the big dog's presence there—it was a herd dog, and in spite of the commotion it was doing a country fair job of keeping those critters corraled on the lowered ramp. Fleetingly, Hawke wondered where the dog's master was. In the second car where the ramp had been only partially lowered at the time of the blast, the tightly packed cattle were frenziedly rocking the car back and forth as if it were caught in a high wind. The train man holding the rope loosed for lowering the ramp dangled at the end of it, marionettelike, in a grim effort to keep from falling beneath the battering of the frenzied beasts. Hawke could have told the man he was fighting a losing battle.

The shine of his black knee boots dulled, his black clothes coated in a heavy layer of dust, Hawke made a dash for the baggage car at about the same time as the railroad detectives. Hawke, intent on one goal, was unaware of the presence of either Tom Fisher or Will Barnett. Hawke's one thought was to get the money and clear out before all the ruckus settled down and folks started taking serious note of what was happening around them. The last thing he wanted or needed right now was some heroic passenger attempting to stop a train robbery. Hawke never had been able to figure out why folks got into such a state over money that was not even theirs.

For a split second Hawke paused by the tightly closed door to the baggage car while pondering the possibilities of what waited for him within. Had any or all of his gang already forced their way in, or had they grouped somewhere out of sight for the assault and he was the first? The bellowing of the cattle issuing from the stock cars was not lessening; in fact, he could swear it was still growing louder. The cars were making shuddering, creaking sounds as they swayed on their wheels, and the clank of the metal wheels against the tracks sent the animals into an even wilder frenzy.

As Hawke reached for the door to the baggage car, he glanced upward, spotting the pair of men heading his way, coming across the top of the cars. What had made him look up Hawke did not know, but he was grateful to whatever Fate had caused him to do it. In a low crouch, the men were plainly trying to approach unseen as they moved swiftly, unhesitatingly, over the first couple of cars. It was the pitching and tossing cattle cars that gave them pause before, aware now of Hawke's gaze fastened on them, they plunged determinedly ahead. When Hawke saw the guns come out, he knew they were more than just concerned passengers. The incongruity of their sudden appearance stalled Hawke in his tracks for a moment, staring as the odd pair tried to maintain their footing on the top of the pitching car while they swung their gun barrels to bear on him. The roof of the faded-red cattle car pitched beneath their feet like a ship at sea and the continuing bellows of the cattle rose with the ferocity of a storm engulfing its craft.

The split-second pause was enough for Hawke. Instinctively he dove for the ground. Then he started scrambling under the shelter of the baggage cars, barking his shins on the rails as the guns went off, peppering the earth in his wake simultaneously with a small explosion within the baggage car directly above him. A puff of smoke shot downward through the floorboards into Hawke's face. Pronto had blown the safe. The money was theirs! Scrambling over the tracks, Hawke craned his neck to see if all was clear before emerging on the far side of the car. Metal shrieked and groaned, wood splintered, cattle bellowed, and something hit the ground with a shuddering crash.

Hawke jerked with a start, whacking his head against the baggage car's undercarriage, then rolled back to peer out at the havoc raging about the train. Dazed, he could vaguely hear women screaming and men swearing, the sound coming from the front passenger car. And he thought he detected a strain at the linkage of the baggage car to the cattle car directly in front of it. Then he craned his neck a bit more and got the full blast of the bizarre scene outside his protective cave. Cattle were everywhere, bellowing and trampling anything in their path. The odd dog that had attempted to keep Ringo for an old bone was going berserk trying to round them up and herd them in the direction they were supposed to be taking. The stock car closest to the baggage car was tipped at a peculiar angle, half over and off the tracks. The whole side of it where the train man had been trying to hold the unloading gate closed was splintered, the gate broken entirely off, and the man was cowering beneath the remains of the car much the same as Hawke was huddled beneath the baggage car. Up ahead, the foremost stock car was completely over on its side, half pulling the passenger car over with it.

The shots the two strangers on top of the stock car had fired had been the last straw, and Hawke got some satisfaction from seeing them clinging to the tilted stock cars, guns nowhere in sight, in their desperate effort not to fall to the ground and risk the hoofs of the panicked beasts. Until Hawke saw something else out of the corner of his eye, he was enjoying the scene. The dog had chased at least a dozen head of cattle around the ramshackle shack in a valiant effort to control them, but when they appeared at the other side the horses, hidden there for the gang's escape, were running ahead of the cattle, eyes rolling, whinnies of panic sharp and piercing. It did not look as if they were likely to stop running this side of the Rio Grande.

Jumping up, Hawke banged his head a second painful time, scrunched down, rolled from under the train, and threw open the baggage car's doors, his eyes settling immediately on his men.

They had their guns out, the only thing that kept them from looking entirely like a bunch of schoolboys caught with their hands in the rock candy. A railroad employee lay in the far corner, bound and gagged, no one paying him much attention while Pronto muttered under his breath, punctuating his speech with curses, for everyone to hurry up. Hart Jackson was patiently holding open a large sack while the others stuffed in the money, Pronto moving like a man possessed. Ringo and Rawlins were half counting the money as they placed it lovingly into the bag.

"Didn't you pack of idiots post any kind of watch?" Hawke demanded.

Pronto grinned. "Kind of figured you was doin' the watchin'."

"I did," Hawke sputtered. "I watched a crazy dog and well over a dozen cattle run our horses off! And I watched what had to have been a couple of railroad detectives who knew what we were doing and tried to pick me off on my way over here."

"Must 'a been quite a show," Hart Jackson quipped with a roughish grin.

"Get your tails moving before you get 'em caught in a crack!" Hawke bellowed, losing patience as he was confronted with the irksome fact that there was only one way out for them now: the engine.

It was the only answer. Without their horses, they could not very well hike out on foot, and the train's engine would provide the necessary transportation they needed as well as stranding those connected with the train. Since he and the railroads had never gotten along, Hawke had long since made it his business to know how to handle the different types of engines now on the tracks. And this was one of the old ones, one of those he knew best.

Hawke took the lead as he slipped out of the baggage car on the west side, away from the shack and the prying eyes that had seen them pass that way once before. Some of the chaos was quieting, the cattle having now scattered a goodly distance, the dog in pursuit, the railroad man surveying the damage to the cars, and the two detectives, freed from their tenacious perch, instigating a minute search for Hawke and his followers—or leaders, depending on how one cared to look at the situation as it stood. Crouched low, they started to edge along the length of the train as Hawke had indicated.

Hawke and his men had barely passed the remnants of the splintered cattle car when a commotion broke out behind them, near the baggage car. The man they had left tied up had to have attracted attention somehow. And when he told the others what had happened, the whole train would be after them.

There was no longer any need for stealth, only speed. Throwing caution aside, Hawke and his men sprinted for the engine, making no attempt at a dignified boarding. George Rawlins saw to the disconnecting of the engine from the rest of its cars while Hawke and the others hit the steps in a pack and ran smack into the engineer wielding a stout piece of cordwood as a club. The engineer had evidently been expecting something like this since the twin, strangely placed explosions. He staggered toward them enraged, swinging his club. Hawke nimbly sidestepped as Jackson's hand shot forward, snagging the man's shirtfront in an iron grasp, and easily launched him in a somersaulting arch off the platform to the hard earth. The engineer landed hard and rolled, staggering to his feet again, heading determinedly back toward the engine.

The pressure gauge was low—Hawke spotted it immediately. The engineer was a canny man. In anticipation of something such as this happening he had allowed it to drop. Now it would give him time to try to retake the engine. Until the steam was built up again the engine could not move.

Hawke swore under his breath. "Feed the fire, Pronto," he yelled as Rawlins swung on board barely ahead of the irate engineer, who was bellowing like a wounded bear. Rawlins grinned companionably as the railroad man mounted the steps, then almost casually placed a boot in the center of his chest and sent him sprawling backward into the dirt once again.

"Think you better hurry things up a mite," Rawlins drawled. "It 'pears like we're about to have more company." He pointed vaguely in a direction beyond where both Pronto and Ringo were madly feeding the engine's fire to where a small knot of men had gathered, and with a pair in the lead were headed their way.

Hawke would have liked nothing better than to have been able to follow Rawlins' advice, but the needle on the gauge was just beginning to creep toward the red line, indicating the metal monster was starting to build up a head of steam. As he craned his neck to peer around Pronto and Ringo's sweating and straining exertions, he saw the guns. The pair he had earmarked as working for the railroad had managed to somehow find and retrieve their weapons. Hawke did not like it. He could use a gun better than most, but he hated to resort to it. He had no desire to kill anyone, not even what was probably a pair of detectives out for the hides of him and his men. Hawke had killed before, when his life had hung in the balance, but the posters out on Salvador Hawke and his bunch made no mention of murder, and he intended to keep it that way. If he dropped one of the fearless twosome out there in his tracks, Hawke was sure the railroad would press for murder, and that would bring the bounty hunters like flies to a dead carcass.

Sweat was gathering on Hawke's forehead as he manipulated the controls, anxiously checking the bank of gauges that confronted him. Only a few seconds more, a few seconds, and they would pull away. He did not think the men coming toward the trains were aware of the fact that the engine had been uncoupled from the rest of the train. They would find out soon enough.

"Hey look!" Jackson stood at Hawke's elbow, his hard, angular face genuinely puzzled. "Now what do you think they're up to?" He set the stack of money down on top of the tender and stared out the sides.

The men who had been coming toward the engine in a body had suddenly split, one of the pair of leaders at the head of one group, the other with the other half. Hawke had gotten a fairly good look at the pair doing the organizing, and vowed not to forget them. One was tall, with a cowpuncher's build, brown hair, a grim, pinched mouth and small pig eyes. The other was more heavyset but shorter, with gray-streaked black hair and a weasel look about him. They fit pretty well the descriptions he had gotten through his sources of the detectives the railroad had hired to run them to ground. There was supposed to be a third one, though, and his absence puzzled Hawke a little, but only a

little. He had neither the time nor the inclination to ponder why
there were only two men out there waving guns around trying to
nail his hide to the barn door instead of three. Right now he was
more concerned with the way the ones he knew about were
slinking around the train trying to come up on their blind side.

"Oh hell," Rawlins muttered softly as he threw the engineer
off the side again, the man swearing a blue streak and vowing all
kinds of mayhem to be committed upon them if he ever got his
hands on them.

"Give it up!" a nasal voice full and raspy called to them.
"Throw down your guns and climb down. We've got you surrounded."

George Rawlins gave a slow, lazy smile, Jackson shrugged,
and Hawke swore bitterly, banging his fist brutally against the
gauge that was creeping slowly up the red line. Abruptly the
gauge's little black needle popped up to the red line as Pronto
and Ringo continued to frantically heave wood into the fire.

"This is your last chance!" the voice warned. "Throw your
guns down and climb out!"

Hawke released the brake and threw the throttle forward. For
an instant, nothing, then metal wheels spun frantically against
metal track, seeking to gain a purchase, and the engine lurched
forward with a sharp jerk and a shrieking groan of protesting
steel.

"Stop that train!" The authoritative voice that had commanded them before broke thinly above the lurching, clanging
start of the old engine.

Rawlins bent to lend Ringo and Pronto a hand with the wood,
but quickly realized three in so tightly confined an area did more
to hinder than help, and for the moment withdrew as the well-
oiled pair kept up the co-ordinated effort. The engine was moving now, though slowly. A gun cracked sharply above the rattling creaks of the creeping engine. The bullet whanged past
Hawke's ear, bounced above his head, and tore Rawlins' sleeve
before burying itself in the wood pile.

With a jerk, Rawlins' gun came out, but the engine was already starting to pick up speed. The wind whistled around them,

guns cracked from behind, and the fire burned high, its orange flames licking in a wild frenzy at the fuel it was fed in huge amounts. Rawlins glowered for a few moments, his brown eyes unusually stormy, ready to exchange lead with anyone who cared to try him, but the engine now was pulling away from its pursuers far too quickly to allow for accurate shooting. The barking of the guns faded behind them, muffled by the wind and covered by the engine's mechanical workings.

Hawke began to relax. They had made it, though this time not by much. Bracing an arm in the open square of a window, he leaned out as he had seen many an engineer do in the past, and glanced backward. In the distance small figures were moving around, and the rest of the train, possessing no power to transport itself, sat unmoving on the tracks like a dead dinosaur. Hawke saw something else as well, something fluttering out in a long stream behind them on the wind. It appeared to be paper, and the tiny figures behind were leaping about in agitation.

Horrified, Hawke was hit by a sudden insight and looked sharply around. The money bag sat exactly where Jackson had put it on top of the tender, opened, bills being sucked out by the wind of their passage.

"Jackson!" Hawke bellowed so loud the man jumped and the others froze. "The money!" he shouted and started for it, but Jackson jerked around and grabbed it first, hastily pulling the drawstring closed on the top.

Hawke, not even wanting to think about how much they had lost, turned to what he had been doing. He could have sworn a blush of red had suffused Jackson's dark cheeks as he had faced the others. No understanding or forgiveness had flashed on Ringo or Pronto's sweating faces that Hawke could see. As for Rawlins, it was hard to tell. The laconic, rawboned Southerner was a tough man to read.

It was beginning to seem almost as if they were jinxed. Hawke was not even sure he wanted to allow the question floating around in his mind to take on clear form. The question he had asked before: What else could go wrong?

CHAPTER 2

The engine stood still, puffing like a belabored beast while Hawke's men piled off. Its fires were high, the steam up. One last time Hawke checked the gauges, then released the brake and again threw the throttle forward. The engine began to roll under him, and Hawke threw a few extra pieces of wood into the roaring fire before stepping to the side and jumping to the ground as the engine continued to pick up speed quickly. He had brought the engine to the point closest, cross-country, to their hideout. And where hopefully their horses would have returned. From here they had to walk, and Hawke expected the sour looks that greeted him when he picked himself up after an impressive roll terminating his jump from the now rapidly moving engine.

Hart Jackson still clutched the money bag in his fist, and while no one had made a move to relieve him of it, they glowered at him and muttered uncomplimentary remarks.

"Damned horses," Pronto fumed as he stomped along in his high-heeled riding boots. "Damned spooky critters. If it weren't for them none 'a this would'a happened."

Hawke could not debate that. In fact, he was in no mood to debate anything. A long walk lay ahead of them. Near fifteen miles as close as he could figure, and they would be needing all the breath they had for that. The sound of the train's engine puffing and rattling could be heard farther and farther off in the distance. He had no idea how far it would go before it stopped, but he hoped it would not get there very soon.

Because they had pulled the plug on the water-storage tank, the engine had not been able to take on much water at the stop. A bit earlier Hawke had worried that the thing would boil dry and lose steam. Now, though, he hoped it would, and the miserable machine would never be the same.

Salvador Hawke was not a man basically set against machines of all kinds. None could accuse him of being opposed to progress. He had proper respect for other men's accomplishments, and if the truth be known, he did not hate the railroad trains nearly as nuch as he hated the railroad men and the mentality behind the entire operation. Far too many of their number preached that the end justified the means. Hawke realized that what he and his men did was in no way a major impediment to the railroads, but it did put money in the pockets of himself and his men. And at the same time he remained as an irritating bee continually buzzing around the heads of the railroad's big brass.

This time, though, Hawke was not sure the return, the gratification, had been worth the risk, even if the money definitely had. They had come much too close, and it was not over yet. A posse would be after them for sure, and they had better be well out of sight by the time it was organized. But Hawke was not really worried. Sending the engine on ahead of where they had gotten off was a nice touch. It would take a posse days to pinpoint the exact spot, if they managed it at all. Jackson was seeing to their back trail, and the half of him that was Indian did a good job of erasing signs. His skill had pulled them out of a hole a time or two in the past.

The problem was, Hawke reflected as they continued to walk, that things were no longer going right for them. There had to be a better way. He did not plan on giving up his career. Why, over the past couple of years he had seen things and heard things that he would have put off to some mountain man's yarn-spinning if he had not seen, at first hand, a great part of the changes that were coming. There was no getting away from it: They were going to have to do some changing themselves if they wanted to survive. And that instinct, Hawke figured, was about the strongest instinct among them: survival.

As they plodded along, Hawke continued to ponder the situation. There seemed never to be any easy answers. Maybe Pronto had been right in his ravings. Maybe the main problem was the spooky horses. If they had not run off, they would not have been in the fix they found themselves in. They also would not have found it necessary to walk many miles in rugged terrain wearing boots made for riding. Horses had been known to pull up lame and to run themselves to death, again leaving riders on foot. But for this kind of country, what else was there? It was a knotty problem, but Hawke's aching feet were demanding he find a solution for it, and fast.

When they finally reached the small cabin hidden in the trees the next day, they found their horses grazing quietly in the small meadow below—all of them, that was, except Ringo's horse, which had always been a laggard and a loner and would probably be turning up soon. Almost in unison the heads of the horses came up at the sight of the men approaching on foot, and while the beasts appeared interested in their arrival they did not seem overly eager to greet them.

After trudging many weary miles and spending a cold, uncomfortable night on the trail without supplies, Salvador Hawke was in no mood for games as he went to his horse. As he came up on the suddenly skittish animal he noted with disgust that the saddle he had taken such pains with, soaping and softening it over past months since he had gotten it, looked as if it had been dragged through the brush and tromped in the dust. With a sigh, Hawke started to swear under his breath and reached for the reins. With a wild look in its eye, the horse's head jerked up and it took a couple of stiff-legged backward steps before Hawke's advance. Apparently the animal had enjoyed its brief taste of freedom, and though it had headed home by instinct it did not seem to be planning on giving up entirely without a fight.

Hawke swore with a little more enthusiasm as he noted that Rawlins walked up to his steed and led it away, docile at the end of its reins, as if just the adventure had been enough for it. Pausing, Hawke watched as his horse's ears flicked back and forth at the sound of his voice and by its stance proved ready to bolt. Hawke waited, not patiently, as the others, save Ringo, who stayed to watch, collected their mounts and trudged up to the cabin.

"Give me a hand," Hawke called out to Ringo. "I don't want to wind up chasing this jughead all over the countryside."

Ringo nodded and started moving around behind the horse while the animal swung partway around to watch his progress, its attention divided now between the two men. Hawke paused while Ringo advanced. Nostrils flaring, the horse tossed its head, ears pricked forward, eyes showing mostly white. With head held high it went up on its toes, almost dancing with indecision as to which direction to take. Hawke hesitated. Ringo pressed, and the horse made a dash to be free of both of them.

It was hard to say exactly when the idea came to him, but if prodded, Hawke would have had to admit it was when he grabbed for those reins as his horse shot past him and he found himself sprawled face down in the dirt, grasping empty air as the animal frolicked a few yards off, tossing its mane and tail, whinnying triumphantly and encouraging a second try. Hawke's lips pressed closed on dirt and his teeth ground grit as he levered himself upright and glared after the errant beast, another sight, one he had seen a few months before, occupying his mind. The answer to their problems had been there all the time but they had been too blind, too set in their ways to see it. This was a new century, the world was moving forward. They would have to do the same. And he had seen the answer right there in front of him when they had been in Denver.

Strolling over, Ringo squatted down beside Hawke, barely suppressing a grin, gazing at him steadily from amused gray eyes. "You gonna try it again? Maybe we could try some kind 'a diversion this time."

"The hell with the horse!" Hawke exploded, leaping to his feet and storming off in the direction of their cabin.

Slowly Ringo unkinked his legs and stood up, gazing after Hawke's retreating back. He sure had his dander up over something. And Ringo hoped it was not something he had done or said. Nobody liked to get on Hawke's bad side, that black side of his nature that housed and nurtured murderous intent. It was not a good place, for man or beast, to be. Ringo glanced over his shoulder at Hawke's horse. The animal seemed puzzled, even distressed, that Hawke had simply walked off without him. It shook its head a little uncertainly and eyed Ringo with a suspicious air, as if the whole thing could be a trick, a charade to catch him off his guard.

Ringo looked at the horse and shook his head very slowly. "Now you went and done it," he said ominously. "Now you really went and done it."

The horse nickered softly as Ringo too turned his back and began to walk away, following in Hawke's wake to see what was going on. Hawke's behavior had seemed a bit strange lately, but then everything they had done had seemed to turn out a little strange for quite some time. What they were going to do about it remained the seemingly insoluble question.

Behind him, Ringo could hear the soft tread of the horse's hoofs as the animal ambled along, dragging the reins across the ground, curious now as to why he had suddenly found himself alone in the middle of the meadow and he had been left to his own devices, when all his fellows were together in a tight bunch before the cabin.

"Pronto was right," Ringo heard Hawke saying as Ringo closed the door behind him and leaned up against the wall to listen.

Every head in the room turned in Pronto's direction. Both proud and puzzled, Pronto looked a bit uncomfortable with his suddenly elevated status, and everyone else looked uncertain. Pronto was rarely right. Also, Hawke had not yet stated exactly what the Frenchman was right about.

"It was the horses," Hawke went on, "the horses that were our problem. We need something more dependable."

"Naw," Rawlins objected, brown eyes brooding, "they was just scared is all. Can't tell me you wouldn't 'a been scared yourself with all them there cattle runnin' at you. Our bunch are good critters," he added, a certain amount of fondness creeping into his tone.

"But they did spook," Hawke pointed out. "They did run off and leave us with one foot on the shore and the other on the boat with the tide going out. We need something we know is going to be there waiting when we're done, and"—Hawke paused dramatically—"I know what it is."

"What?" Rawlins groused, not looking up. "Only thing you know is gonna be there when you want 'em is your feet. You plan to start runnin'?"

The others looked from Hawke to Rawlins and back again, waiting. Hart Jackson looked highly amused, his soft brown eyes twinkling with humor. Ringo was interested but doubtful, and Pronto, for a change, just kept his mouth shut.

By the time Hawke spoke again all of them were waiting tensely for his next words. He, though, was not going to make it too easy for them. "We saw them, all of us, when we were in Denver," Hawke went on. "They were right there at the fair looking us in the face, but none of us knew what we were looking at."

"Goddammit!" Pronto finally exploded. "What the hell did we see? What're you talking about?"

"A contraption!" Hawke informed them dramatically. "A twentieth-century contraption. The fella called it a motorcycle."

They all fell silent, gazing at one another with blank looks. None remembered such a thing as Hawke remembered.

"I'll stick with the horses," Rawlins drawled.

"What'd it look like?" Jackson asked.

Hastily Hawke described the new mode of transportation he was exhorting, the bicycle shape with the longer body, the engine and the controls on the handlebars.

"And," Hawke went on quickly, "it don't have to eat and drink like a horse, don't pick up stones in its hoofs or go lame, it'll be right where you left it when you come back, and those things cover more miles in a couple of hours than we can in a whole day of hard riding. No posse ever formed would have a chance of keeping up with us."

"Yea, but in the race between the turtle and the rabbit," Rawlins said philosophically, "it was the turtle that won."

"All of you know," Hawke reminded them, "that things ain't been going too well lately." He looked meaningfully from one man to another, meeting each one's gaze square. "This is going to work. This is going to change our luck," he declared. "I'm going to use the money we got from the train to buy the motorcycles."

"What about Mrs. McClary?" Pronto asked, reminding Hawke of their promise to the widow to get her enough money to pay the debt her late husband had left on the property, leaving her vulnerable to eviction by the railroad to whom the debt was owed and for whom her husband had worked.

"We'll give her the money we promised her first." Hawke revised his plans. "Then use what's left to buy the motorcycles."

"Why can't we just keep the money and steal them motorcycles you're talking about?" Jackson asked. "I've got me this little gal over in Trinidad. . . ."

"No," Hawke instantly vetoed the idea. "We don't want to draw any more attention to ourselves until after we have the motorcycles. We're going to lay low for a while."

"Lay low!" Pronto bounded to his feet, his black eyes flashing against the starkness of his angular face. "We never layed low before!" he exclaimed, as if it were the ultimate indignity.

"Only a fool couldn't see with the run of luck that we've had that we should pull in our horns and let things cool down for a spell," Hawke reasoned.

"We can't stay here," Jackson put in. "It would take a bit 'a time, but a posse, determined enough, could track us to the door."

Hawke nodded. "We'll move north, set up a camp in the high country. You can cover our trail from here."

Rawlins shook his head. "I'll go with you, but I'm stickin' with the horses."

"How long we gonna hide in some hole like a bunch 'a whipped dogs?" Pronto demanded.

"Just long enough," Hawke replied blandly, well aware of Pronto's famous itchy feet. He never liked to stand in one place too long. It was a problem Hawke had never had to face with the man, since they had never stood still long enough in the past to even let him start to think about moving contrary to Hawke's orders.

"Even a snake knows when to hunt a hole," Rawlins put in. "Like I said before, I'm with you."

"Count me in," Ringo went along while Pronto stomped the

floor and muttered under his breath, waving his arms around like he was attempting to swat flies.

Hawke watched from beneath lowered lids. He had made his position clear, and the others stood with him, if in an admittedly loose fashion. Pronto was their dynamite man, the only one among them who really knew what he was doing with the stuff. Hawke would hate to lose him, especially in the light of Ringo's less than quick grasping of the art.

"All right," Pronto said at last, the decision a weighty one for him in spite of the fact that he made it in his usual manner: fast. "I'll stick, and I'll even try one of your damn motorcycles."

Hawke gave a sage nod of his head as if he had known that would be Pronto's answer in the end all along. "You take the money to the widow McClary." Hawke started counting the money out of the canvas sack, addressing Pronto over his shoulder as he did. "By the time you get back we'll be ready to pull out."

Stuffing the money in a pants pocket, Pronto nodded and strode quickly out the door. Hawke watched through the window as in an offhanded manner Pronto grabbed the reins Hawke's horse still dangled, looped them around the hitching post alongside the others, then mounted his own horse and rode off.

Frowning, Hawke went back to counting the money. It was difficult to try to figure what they were going to need. The price of something as foreign as a motorcycle was totally unknown to him. He did not think it would be arrived at the same way as one did in a horse trade. Denver. He would have to go back to Denver to track the machines down. Then, when he had them, ship them by rail somewhere he and the boys could easily pick them up without drawing too much attention. It would be better if they were nowhere in evidence when he did the actual buying. The idea of shipping them by rail amused Hawke when he paused to think about it. The railroad would be delivering the newest, most modern method of robbing them into the hands of the most-sought, least-seen gang west of the great Mississippi. Hawke liked the idea. Maybe this was what they needed, a vacation and a fresh start. After the years they had put in together, they were probably getting stale, and, he had to admit, apprehensive. Those railroad detectives were good, and they had gotten too close for comfort. Hawke did not even want to ponder how they had known he and his men would be stopping that particular train.

Resuming his counting, Hawke realized that the accident with the money on top of the tender had not left them with much. At least not compared to loot gathered from trains at other times. But it would be enough. Hawke intended to see to that.

CHAPTER 3

Reins dangled loosely from Salvador Hawke's hands where he sat on top of the wagon three months to the day after ordering the newfangled machines, the motorcycles. The train was already well overdue at the station in Santa Fe. For the special occasion, Hawke had hired a wagon. The crates containing the machinery would be heavy, but the horses that stood patiently in the harnesses were up to the job. Stout draft horses, they were sleek and alert, ready for the signal to use the muscles that stood out all over their bodies in glossy ripples. Over the years Hawke had trained his ear to pick out distant train sounds, and he was aware of them now. Distant still, but approaching at a steady rate, the train would be there soon.

His black, broad-brimmed hat pulled down low over his blue eyes, Hawke smiled faintly, enjoying the irony of having the railroad deliver what was destined to be the newest tools of their trade, the brand-new, just barely in production Indian motorcycle. Rawlins, of course, was still unconvinced, but Hawke was confident of winning him over once they put the machines into use. Most people, it seemed, were hesitant to try something new, but once others made use of the product they were usually won over. Hawke hoped Ringo would get back from the saloon before the train arrived. He did not want to have to go get him. One beer to cut the dust and ease the wait should not have taken this long.

From beneath the hat brim low over his eyes, Hawke kept a wary eye out for any sign of trouble. No wanted posters were out on him in this territory to Hawke's immediate knowledge, but the railroads had a long arm. There was no telling where those two detectives who had almost foiled their last robbery would turn up again. Life, Hawke had to admit, *was* getting more difficult. Either that, he decided with a sigh, or he was finally beginning to get old. Considering what he would shortly be taking delivery of, Hawke preferred to believe it was the changing times.

Again he threw a glance in the direction of the saloon, but there was still no sign of Ringo. Hawke was beginning to be sorry he had brought anyone along. Having someone accompany him had seemed like a wise decision at the time, but that had been before he had realized he would be stuck with Ringo. Rawlins had wanted no part of it, and Hart Jackson had gone off hunting the night before. Pronto had been in one of his more dark and aggressive moods, not the best time to take him into a town full of people. The simple process of elimination had left him with an ebullient Ringo, itching for the town life they were not to see. The intent had been that they were to drive straight to the railroad station and take delivery of the large wooden crates before curious onlookers would have time to wonder what was packed in them.

The problem with Ringo had arisen when it became clear that the train was going to be more than just a few minutes late. He had decided on a beer after they had been sitting there waiting for the train only a few minutes. Hawke had been unable to do anything to stop him short of raising just the kind of disturbance he wanted to avoid right now.

Out of the corner of his eye, Hawke caught sight of the sheriff heading his way. Concentrating on his casual pose, Hawke let the reins dangle even looser in his hands as he stretched a leg to ease a cramp and expose his gun to his grasp. Where the hell was Ringo? Hawke swore under his breath. If he had to leave town in a hurry, he was flat going to leave Ringo on his own. Warily he watched as the sheriff approached and stopped before him not more than a foot from the wagon, looking up at Hawke with a pensive air. Hawke continued to gaze straight ahead blankly as if daydreaming while waiting for the train's arrival. Slowly, calmly, the sheriff was taking his measure, and Hawke knew the man would not like what he saw. Salvador Hawke looked nothing at all like any sodbuster who ever wandered in off the plains headed West. As far as any sheriff was concerned, Hawke's appearance spelled out gambler, outlaw, or maybe drummer, and that last one was not very likely. In addition, the first two were not very near to any sheriff's heart. It was sort of like having a snake in the henhouse. Hawke waited, making no effort to speak first.

"Mister," the sheriff said in quiet greeting with a curt nod of his head.

Hawke jerked his head around as if just becoming aware of the sheriff's presence when his voice broke his revelry. "Sheriff," Hawke returned pleasantly, shifting his gaze with intent interest down the length of empty track.

"Train's running a mite late," the sheriff commented. "You might be waiting here quite a spell."

"Don't reckon it'll be much longer," Hawke returned easily. "Don't mind waiting anyhow."

The sheriff nodded slowly as if Hawke had spilled forth pearls of wisdom, and shifted his position to try to get a better look at the stranger seated in the wagon. Just as easily Hawke shifted, attempting to keep the shadow and part of the brim of his hat covering a good portion of his face. He did not plan on making it too easy for the sheriff to get a good look.

Almost the instant he had spotted the sheriff heading in his direction, Hawke had taken the man's measure. The sheriff was of medium build with heavy shoulders, a thick neck, and a determined set to his jaw. The eyes were what had put Hawke on his guard. Piercing and probing, they weighed what they saw as if searching for something.

"You waiting for something on that train? Or maybe someone?" The sheriff appeared to be making conversation, but Hawke was all too aware that he was probing, digging.

"Farm equipment," Hawke felt the words roll easily off his tongue and was surprised they had come so easily. He looked about as much like a farmer as a tumbleweed resembled a rose.

A long silence followed, accented by the sheriff tilting his head in such a way as to appear to be sniffing the air. Then he cleared his throat with noisy effort and grunted "uh-huh" in a tone that left no doubt as to what part of Hawke's statement he believed.

Hawke kept his silence and waited. The train was visible now, puffing down the track toward the station.

"You got any papers for this here farm equipment you're supposed to be collecting here today?" The sheriff leaned casually against Hawke's wagon, confident he had found grounds to send this stranger packing and get a load off his mind. There was something about him and his companion, now nowhere in evidence, he had not liked from the moment they had driven that wagon into town.

The sheriff glanced over his shoulder toward the saloon. The other one had gone in there, and now he was headed back. That made everything a whole lot easier. He could send both of them packing.

Without a word, Hawke reached inside his black jacket to the pocket sewn inside and handed over the necessary papers needed to claim his freight.

Concealing his surprise well, the sheriff accepted the papers from Hawke's hands and began what appeared to be a low, thorough perusal of them. His eyes, though, hardly focused on the words that marched across the papers in neat rows. He was not interested in any freight papers, but the wagon's driver had produced them and he had to at least appear to be looking them over. What interested him the most was the fact that the stranger had papers to present. It did not fit the picture the sheriff had put together of this man and the one who had ridden in with him atop the stout wagon. He knew their faces from somewhere and in his book that probably meant they were wanted. He had shuffled through the posters in his office and come up empty. Still, there was something.

Ringo almost bounced up behind the sheriff as the train pulled into the station, and Hawke knew he had had more than one beer. The sly grin that slid up one side of his smooth round face was a dead giveaway.

"Sheriff," Ringo said thickly in greeting, "nice day, in't it?" He raised his hat a bit from his head, the sunlight shooting through his hair with the starkness of the first winter snowfall.

In the distance, Hawke could hear a dog barking. Ever since the day when they wound up stealing the engine, dogs barking had made him nervous. Nothing could go wrong here, he reminded himself. He was conducting honest business. Picking up what he had already paid for, including the freight costs.

For the moment Ringo had the sheriff's full attention, and Hawke used the opportunity to pull the wagon forward to where they were throwing open the doors of one of the boxcars preparing to unload some crates.

"You want to give us a hand here?" Hawke called to Ringo after he had set the wagon brake and swung aboard to help unload the heavy crates.

"Sure thing, Hawke!" Ringo bellowed loud enough for the entire county to hear.

At the use of his name, Hawke cringed as Ringo headed his way, his step springy, the silly grin still pasted across his face. Hawke, as he lent his hands to helping with the unloading, glanced uneasily at the sheriff. The man was staring openly now. The name had rung a bell. Hawke unloaded the second crate with Ringo standing in the wagonbed to guide it into place beside the first. What was the sheriff going to do? There were no posters out on them in this territory, and the sheriff did not represent the railroad. Hawke continued to work steadily. Rationally, there was nothing the sheriff could do. But then many were the times when lawmen were not known to be rational.

When Hawke turned back to the railroad men helping him unload, he saw they were scrutinizing him with the same intensity as the sheriff. A couple of people standing in the street nearby were also staring at them with curiosity. Ringo and his big mouth. There might not be any posters out on them here, but anyone attached to the railroad would know the names of Hawke and Ringo.

Continuing with what he was doing, Hawke finally got down to the huge drums of fuel that had been included in his shipment. He and Ringo completed the loading alone. The sheriff had drifted nearer again, his gaze steady on the crates and their prominent markings that identified them simply as machinery. That he was trying to peer between the narrow cracks in the crates was plain. Hawke doubted that he would know what he was looking at if he managed to get a good look at them, but he had no intention of spending any more time in town than was necessary.

"Sheriff," Hawke said easily, his tone friendly as he touched his hat brim in the man's direction and snapped the reins over the horses' backs while Ringo still stood in the wagonbed along with the new motorcycles.

The sheriff nodded in reply as he looked critically down at the wagon wheels, which seemed to have sunk a good way in the dust since taking on the load. The horses leaned into their traces, digging their hoofs into the earth to get the load rolling. Muscles stood out starkly beneath glossy hides, and necks bowed with effort as the wagonbed seemed to sag, and the sturdy boards creaked with strain.

More people arrived constantly to stand around and stare at the heavily laden wagon and the two men who manned it. The people kept a respectful distance, but there could be no mistaking the fact that his name was known in this town. Averting his eyes, Hawke kept his eyes focused straight ahead, keeping a tense watch from the corners of his eyes as he drove the wagon at a sedate pace out of town.

Santa Fe was not a dirt-pit little settlement. With a population of over four thousand there were plenty of eyes to follow Hawke's progress along the street as Ringo, comfortably settled among the crates in back, burst into a low, soulful rendition of "Dixie." The team pulled with steady power. Children and dogs seemed to materialize out of thin air and followed him along, the children, mostly boys, keeping to the sides of the street, the dogs yapping at the heels of the placid draft horses. Hawke was not surprised when he caught sight of the sheriff walking briskly along the wooden walkway that ran parallel to his course. The man wore a puzzled expression, still splitting his attention between Hawke and the load his wagon carried. It was hard to tell if the sheriff was just making sure they did not stop anywhere on their way out of town or if the innocent-appearing crates interested him that much. If Hawke had felt he could allow himself the luxury of a smile, he would have grinned at the sheriff. Obviously the sheriff was planning on taking no action of his own, or he would have done it already. But Hawke knew that in days to come the sheriff would remember this day. The day when Salvador Hawke and Ringo had picked up the motorcycles in his town at his train station and he had stood by watching with the rest of the gaping citizens. Hawke watched the sheriff fade in the distance and blend with the flow of the old adobes until he was enveloped and disappeared.

Salvador Hawke would not have felt so smug, nor felt so much like grinning had he been able to, in fact, interpret the sheriff's thoughts accurately. The name Ringo had blurted out had rung a bell for the sheriff, all right, and it had done even more than that. But the sheriff had only limited powers and there was not even a local poster out on Hawke and his strange bunch. The sheriff had gotten a telegram, not too long before, from a U.S. marshal by the name of Liam Cook, trying to get a lead on Hawke's bunch. Before he went to the telegraph office and sent out a message to Marshal Cook, the sheriff was making sure Hawke was clear of his town. The information would be interesting to Cook as well as the railroad people, considering the fact that Hawke and his bunch had been known to have gone to ground after their last strike against the railroad, disappearing completely. It would give them a starting point. A place to begin looking.

A place to start looking for them was something Hawke was not anxious to give any lawman, or railroad man. But the sheriff's thoughts were his own, and Hawke had no way of knowing them. Even if he had known, there would be nothing he could do about it, save uprooting and moving their hideout to more favorable climes.

Clear of town, and for the moment on a downgrade in the trail, Hawke kept the horses to a steady pace while Ringo, still sprawled out in the back, switched to an off-key rendition of

"The Battle Hymn of the Republic" that would have brought a tear to the composer's eye. Hawke loosed the reins a notch and let the horses pick up speed and build momentum for the climb that lay ahead. Settling back in his seat, he let his gaze wander to the towering Sangre de Cristos, their peaks wrapped in snow, seeming to touch the very heavens. The ride back to their hideout in the mountains was a long one. In spite of Ringo's continuing warblings, Hawke settled back in his seat to enjoy it.

CHAPTER 4

Uncrated, fueled as the instructions had said, and lined up in a row, the five Indian motorcycles glinted in the bright sunlight. Hawke checked and double-checked all the instructions while the other men climbed on and minutely examined the machines —all save Rawlins, who gazed upon the newly arrived Indians with a jaundiced eye and kept his distance, sitting on the stump they had been using for splitting firewood, his long legs stretched out before him, his horse standing complacently behind him.

While Ringo, Pronto, and Hart Jackson started their machines as Hawke had instructed, reveling in the mechanical roar that split the mountain-valley stillness, Hawke strolled to where Rawlins sat, his brown-eyed gaze skeptical.

"You gonna join us?" Hawke asked, fully expecting Rawlins to climb slowly to his feet and saunter to the motorcycle that awaited his hand to roar it to life.

"Nope," Rawlins replied in his usual lazy drawl. "Don't reckon I am."

Somewhat taken aback, Hawke fell silent for a moment, considering. Rawlins had never been in favor of the idea, though he had not said much against it. His flat-out refusal to have anything to do with the new machinery was something Hawke had not expected.

The direct approach, he decided, was the best. "Why not?"

"Well," Rawlins began slowly, prophetically, "if I go along with this, next thing you know somebody will be wanting me to climb into some machine and fly through the air. Don't care for that idea much either. I got me a good horse. Me and him are doing just fine the way we are."

The big chestnut nuzzled Rawlins' neck in apparent appreciation of the man's last remark.

"Never did say I would ride one of those things, if you remember," Rawlins reminded Hawke.

"You didn't tell me you wouldn't," Hawke observed.

Rawlins grinned. "You never asked me head on."

Hawke let his eyes wander heavenward before having them jerked back to something closer to home. As he spoke with Rawlins he had been aware of distant revving of motorcycles, but now he heard the spin of narrow tires on earth, the spitting of small stones, and the rush of air as Pronto put his cycle in gear and sped off, at breakneck speed, down the slope. Rawlins appeared amused while his horse, ears pricked forward, eyes following the progress of the cyclist, was curious. Cringing, Hawke watched as the motorcycle bucked beneath Pronto like a berserk range pony away from a saddle too long. Pronto's frantic calls of "Whoa" reached Hawke all the way back to where he stood with Rawlins.

For the moment, all thoughts of Rawlins' stubbornness were driven from Hawke's mind. Sooner or later the man would have to come around to the ways of progress or be left behind. Hawke did not like to think of that last part. Rawlins was the steadiest man of their bunch. Actually, for the time being, Hawke did not have time to think about it as he took off at a dead run along a course he hoped would intercept Pronto.

"Use the brake!" Hawke yelled, though his words were lost on the wind, his voice drowned out by the mechanical roar of the motorcycles.

Rawlins watched him go, shook his head, and reached out to stroke his horse's muzzle.

"Use the brake!" Hawke bellowed again, racing along after Pronto and his runaway cycle. "Let go of the gas!" Hawke added as an afterthought as Pronto continued his weaving, unsteady course across the breadth of the sloping valley. Rocks loomed up before Pronto as insurmountable mountains, and Hawke began to fear for the well-being of the machine beneath Pronto's hand.

For himself, Hawke had gotten a rudimentary knowledge of the workings of the motorcycles when he had bought them. Even over rough ground he rode with confidence, but it had taken a few rides before he had gotten the knack of it. He had hoped to impart his hard-won knowledge with the same painstaking care it had been imparted to him, but he had forgotten about Pronto. Here was a painful reminder that he should never forget about Pronto.

Behind, Hawke could hear the motors of the other two motorcycles roaring, and Ringo's hoots and yells as he egged Pronto on. Ahead, Pronto was charting an erratic course for the stream that cut across the valley. Hawke grit his teeth and pounded on in pursuit, yelling instructions that Pronto gleefully ignored, clinging to the machine like it was a bucking bronc. From what Hawke could see, Pronto was more off than on, but still he kept going.

Hawke started to swear in rhythm to his choppy run, a feat that soon left him breathless and gasping in Pronto's wake. There was no doubt that Pronto had heard his yelled instructions, but merely had not been interested in listening. Turning a baleful glare in the direction of the two remaining motorcycles and their riders atop the small knoll, Hawke dared either of them to duplicate Pronto's ride. Even from that distance Ringo and Jackson could read the set of Hawke's shoulders, the anger in his stance, and neither one was too eager to follow in Pronto's wheel tracks. There would be hell to pay once Hawke caught up with him, and they all knew it.

Pronto's motorcycle buck jumped a couple more times, then wheezed out over open space as it hit the short drop-off where the creek cut through the valley. The engine roared as the new Indian hung suspended in midair, agonizing seconds dragging by before it touched down on the opposite side of the creek, front wheel first. Hawke cringed when he saw it hit. Pronto's grip on the handlebars was something less than firm, his body, already half off the cycle when the front wheel hit, turned abruptly beneath the sudden impact and sent the whole works crashing into the ground. Somersaulting over the handlebars, Pronto hit the half-muddy, grass-covered earth in a roll. The motorcycle rolled over on its side, sputtered a couple of times, and died.

Unhurt, Pronto bounced to his feet, grinning. Not a trace of the French accent he conjured up for special occasions colored his speech.

"That sure was something," Pronto called out to Hawke's stiff-legged approach. "It's gonna take some fancy riding to tame that critter," Pronto chuckled at his own joke despite the fact that no answering smile showed on Hawke's face.

"Just what the hell do you think you were doing?" Hawke demanded. "I told you before that those machines have to be handled with respect. We've got a lot of money invested in them, as well as a future depending on them!"

"Ain't nothing more than some hunks of metal thrown together," Pronto bristled, getting annoyed at Hawke's attitude. " 'Sides, if I remember right, it was all our money paid for these things. Seems like I should have the right to break mine up if that's what I want to do." He raised himself up to his full five-foot, three-inch height, his black eyes flashing as he strutted back and forth a couple of times with an expression resembling the cock of the walk.

Hawke eyed him silently for a few moments. "If you break this machine up," he imparted the information very slowly and articulately, "you're gonna be looking for a new bunch to run with." Hawke paused. "Now let's pick it up and see if there's any damage."

Irritable, Pronto began muttering under his breath, but did as Hawke told him, lifting the awkward machine from the ground to balance it again on its two wheels.

Rawlins galloped up, riding his chestnut bareback, urging the animal about as close to the machine as it appeared willing to come. "Don't appear likely you'll have to shoot it this time," he said sagely, grinning at Hawke. "Maybe next time."

Hawke shot Rawlins an impatient look, a glance that went right past the mounted man to where the other two cyclists were bringing their machines down the slope at a much more sedate pace. As he watched their progress, Hawke grunted his approval. Then Pronto kicked his wounded machine into life, proving Hawke's worst fears unfounded, and Rawlins snorted, wheeled his horse, and galloped off before the animal had a chance to take exception to the racket and strange appearance of the other oncoming motorcycles. Also, before Hawke made another try at talking him into climbing up on one of those things. Hawke watched Rawlins move off. He would come around in time. Hawke had no doubt of that.

With renewed enthusiasm, Hawke returned to his motorcycle, climbed aboard, and brought it to life. The engine throbbed beneath him like a pulsing heartbeat and the echoes of the growling machines sounded through the valley with an undulating force that set the aspens to quaking on the bordering hillsides. Settling his hat more firmly on his head, Hawke scooted down the hillside to join the others where they were describing circles in the meadow's deep grass and already beginning to attempt to climb low slopes with the unfamiliar machines clamped tightly between their thighs, much as they would a bunch of first-string cow ponies fresh off the range. Hawke watched from one side for a few moments, then gunned his engine and led the way. The others fell in behind him, gliding easily through the grass and taking the low hillside with a little effort. The horses up on the corral by the cabin whinnied at the strange, continuous noises, nervously circling the corral in a tightly packed bunch. They were acting like there was a panther on the prowl somewhere nearby. His own horse tied to the top rail, Rawlins sat astraddle the fence watching, shaking his head in disbelief as Hawke and the others went through their antics. Absently, he would scratch or stroke a questioning muzzle that was stretched tentatively in his direction as he watched the changing scene below.

Rawlins saw Hawke, with an abrupt motion, raise his arm in a broad, sweeping gesture for the others to accompany him and took off for the draw that led to the mouth of the valley and from there led a choked trail to more open country. In an oddly scattered pattern the others fell into line behind Hawke's intense, forceful figure, bent over the machine's handlebars like he was leading troops into battle. As they disappeared down the trail the throb of the engines dimmed, and Rawlins shifted uncomfortably a couple of times waiting for them to reappear, then grabbed the reins and vaulted up on his horse's back. Gripping with his knees and heels, Rawlins rode after them, wondering where they were headed. Trees and earth muffled distant sounds of the engines until the vehicles took on the sound of bees droning in warm summer sunshine. Rawlins did not press his mount. He needed only to reach an overlook to be able to see what in blazes was going on.

Salvador Hawke reveled in the feeling as wind whipped beneath his hatbrim to either side of his face in a stinging caress. Each time was as exhilarating as it had been the first time. Hawke felt he knew the machine now as well as he knew the country surrounding them. And he realized that his men were going to have to ride as if they were glued to the seats of their machines. To be able to do that they were going to have to do more than ride in gentle circles in a broad, wide-open meadow. They all had plenty to learn, as Pronto's demonstrative tumble across the creek had shown him. In Hawke's estimation, there was one sure way to learn, and that was to do. And the best place to do it in this country was just beyond the twin hills that stood guard at the entrance of the trail leading to their stronghold in the Sangre de Cristos. Beyond them was country that turned into mesas, bordered by rolling hills and towering mountains. There were ridges, ledges, drop-offs, and cuts in the surface of the earth that would turn a man's bent to caution even on horseback. Atop a motorcycle the terrain would be an excellent training ground, teaching each one of them to negotiate hazards they would find on the trail. They would have to be prepared for anything. The machines were dependable and swift, Hawke had satisfied himself on that score. But handling them on a rough, steep trail would be a lot different from handling a horse. With the lawmen that bore remembering, Hawke was aware of the fact that each member of their bunch had better be able to straddle the motorcycle as if it were a part of him. As if he had never been taken off the familiar place he had known all his life, his horse's back.

George Rawlins was foremost on Hawke's mind as they threaded their way down the twisting trail toward the chosen training ground. If he did not change his mind soon, he was going to be a real problem. Hawke did not want to lose him, yet how was he going to keep up with the speeding cycles running cross-country on a horse? Hawke had not counted on such an obstacle when he had originated the idea of using the motorcycles to hit the railroads. The others had gone along without much of a fight, while Rawlins had remained silently, seemingly unswervably opposed to the whole idea. Hawke had no doubt as they moved along, the motors buzzing in his ears, snatching away all other sound, that Rawlins was following, watching them. The man would not be able to stand it, just waiting back there at the shack. He would be in the hills somewhere behind them, and Hawke figured they would have to show him that the horses he loved would soon be obsolete.

First there had been the railroad and the bicycle, then the motorcycle. The man who had sold Hawke the Indian motorcycles had sworn that next there would be something called horseless carriages carrying people about. And he had also envisioned the air machines the Rawlins had so prophetically rejected for himself. Hawke did not know if he would go so far as to foresee such a thing, but motorcycles were here now. They were real, and he was sure they were going to prove most useful.

Hawke smiled into the wind that bit at his face and gave the machine beneath him some more gas. It slipped ahead of the others with little urging, catching them all by surprise and sending them after him in an oddly undulating line strung out behind and to the side. He waved them in and they closed formation somewhat, each one still riding stiff as a corpse, a far cry from the relaxed postures they had practiced in the saddle.

From his overlook on the ridge that gave Rawlins a clear view down into the surrounding countryside for miles around, he was the first to spot the girl and the camp, though they were well separated when he picked them out through the trees that attempted to obscure his view. From what he could see, the girl and the camp did not appear to be connected. She was neither riding away from it nor toward it, but rather following a course that would take her past it without ever being aware of the camp's presence. Where she had come from and where she was going, her shimmering blue-black hair whipped out behind her in a sparkling veil as the fine pair of horses that drew her light carriage stepped out briskly, were mysteries. True, there was no longer anything to fear from Indians, probably why they had the gall to name those noisy contraptions after them, but the trails were filled with men of disrepute and she was a woman alone.

The camp must have been a good mile beyond where the woman's carriage would pass, separated from her by a creek rushing within its banks, and a tight cluster of hills that rose up abruptly, goosefleshlike out of the land. Rawlins thought he could make out three men in the distant camp, but that was about all that could be discerned. The men could be there for many reasons, but Rawlins knew the conclusion Hawke would jump to, and probably be right. Men were hunting them, and this was a mighty out-of-the-way place to be setting up a camp without a very good reason.

Off to the right of the strange scene that had met Rawlins' eye when he topped the crest were Salvador Hawke and his Indians, still cut off from view of either the woman or the camp. But even though they were not in sight, it was doubtful that the motorcycles would have gone unheard. The continuous growling roar was bouncing off the hillsides and rolling through the surrounding valleys. In fact, the matched pair of horses that drew the woman's carriage were showing marked signs of increasing nervousness. And, in the camp, there was new activity.

Rawlins' every instinct told him he should be storming down the steep hillside, riding hard to warn Hawke of what he had seen. Of the camp they were headed straight for. The strange, mysterious woman was of small consequence, but the men, and the camp, were well worthy of note. And only a day before this whole area had been deserted. Hart Jackson had scouted it and he would not have missed that camp. Hawke had ridden out believing the area to be all clear for the training exercise. Rawlins would have done it too, if there had been a chance in hell that he could have caught up in time to do any good, but the distance was far too great, and there was no shortcut. So, all things being equal, Rawlins chose discretion and kept his distance. That did not mean that he planned to do nothing at all. Lifting his horse's reins, he nudged the animal with his heels, sending it down the slope at an even pace. He would follow along and see what happened. He had his rifle in his saddle boot, something the others, mounted on the motorcycle contraptions, would not have. Below, Rawlins picked out a hill that would supply him with another spot where he could get a good view of what was happening.

Glancing over his shoulder, Hawke could see the shape of Rawlins and his horse making their way down the steep side of one of the hills that boxed in their valley. He was following along at a distance. Hawke smiled his satisfaction. Perhaps this outing would teach Rawlins something.

Hawke kept to his present course, just giving the men a chance to get used to sitting their machines in rough country. After the initial spill, Pronto had not pulled any more of his tricks, but Hawke was alert for more of them. If he knew Pronto, the man was just waiting for another opportunity to show itself.

Behind him Hawke took note of the others' progress. Ringo had taken a spill of his own a short way back on the narrow trail that led out of the box canyon. Giving the machine too much gas when he had started to scale a slight hill, Ringo had sent himself spilling over backward as the loose rock rolled out from under his back wheel and the front wheel left the ground in response to the power surge and the upward motion. Since then his lips had been set in a grim line, his face drawn in concentration, his eyes fixed on the rocky, uneven trail ahead.

Jackson nearly met a similar fate, but he had already seen both Pronto and Ringo fall, and he relished the experience about as much as getting thrown from an outlaw horse. When he hit the soft spot on the hillside and started his sideways slide, Hart Jackson moved more quickly than the less fortunate Ringo. A stiff right leg locked, stomped into the loose earth like a retaining stake, and brought him up short as the forward momentum had given way to a slide that would have sucked him down the hill in a bone-jarring tangle of limbs and machine. Jackson's strength, always surprising in spite of the well-set squareness of his frame, had been even more appalling during those few seconds when he had seemed to defy gravity, bracing both himself and the heavy machine on a roll of a hillside that had been virtually sliding out from under him. But somehow he had done it, then restarted the stalled motorcycle with about as much aplomb as a finely dressed city fellow out for a Sunday ride astride his most trustworthy mount.

Even farther back, Hawke could still catch sight of Rawlins on occasion. The man had found himself another point from which to observe them—a hill, lower than the steep grade of the one guarding the mouth of their canyon, but still higher than most of the surrounding countryside. He seemed to pause there again for a time, gazing out over the open terrain. Hawke wondered if he was even able to pick them out any longer from among the tangle of low trees they had entered. He doubted it. But then, what was he looking at so intently? His attention appeared to be riveted to something. Rawlins was a hard man to read. He could have spotted a deer on a distant hillside. Hawke preferred to think that might be it.

Up ahead a tight cluster of tree-studded little hills sprung up out of the earth. Hawke chose it as their turn-back point. They would loop the huddled hills and start back for camp. The men had had enough of an experimental ride for one day. It took time for a man to get used to his machine and to relax on it as if he were sitting a rocking-chair saddle. They were not going to do it all in one time out. Also, Rawlins, while he appeared to be following along at a distance, would be forced to get a better look at the ease with which the motorcycles were handled when they were coming back toward him and moving too fast for him to sidestep getting a close-up view. Hawke was bound and determined to win him over. There was a fifth Indian sitting on the hill back at the shack, and he did not intend to let anything keep him from getting Rawlins up on it. He was too good a man to lose just because he was shy of progress. Now that he was more aware of Rawlins' objections he could have another, more serious talk with him when they got back into their walled valley.

Satisfied, Hawke built the speed up a little, causing the others to do the same to keep up, giving them a taste of how fast the new machine could go.

Moving fast, all of them were hunched low over their handlebars when they swooped into the turn rounding the base of the hills, dust flying in the wake of their thundering machines and suddenly came face to face with a lone rider and what was plainly a camp laying within sight behind him. When they spotted him he was still a good twenty-five yards off, but his horse was already wild-eyed and skittish from the strange sounds echoing weirdly off the hills. At the first glimpse of the two-wheeled contraptions, the horse reared, rider clinging determinedly to its back, his seat very definitely not solid.

Hawke's reflexes reacted instantly. Fearing the rider would be thrown, he slammed on the brakes, his motorcycle slewing sideways beneath him in almost a complete circle, throwing up a wide arch of dust and stones in the process. Thrusting one leg out to brace his abrupt halt, he craned his neck around to get a clearer view of the rider, but the rising dust and plunging horse kept him from it as the rest of Hawke's bunch struggled to bring their cycles to a swift halt.

Pronto, attempting to duplicate Hawke's maneuver, felt his machine whip around in a tight circle, then lay down on its side like a wounded horse, the difference being that the motorcycle still kept going, sliding sideways along the ground, dragging Pronto with it. Ringo cut his wheel hard, had more presence of mind than Pronto in that he released the gas, but then forgot the brake, yelling "Whoa" as futilely as Pronto had earlier. Without the lifeblood of gas to propel it, the machine slowed abruptly, but not fast enough to keep Ringo from gracefully falling into the circle his motorcycle had cut, careening into Pronto and sending him sprawling back into the dirt from which he had begun to extricate himself. Hart Jackson, a bit farther to the rear, barely managed to avoid disaster, coming to a halt several feet behind Hawke.

What the hell was that camp doing there anyway? Hawke glanced over his shoulder at Jackson as if for an explanation.

Jackson grinned and shrugged. It had not been there the day before, when he had been out scouting.

The rider of the horse was still clinging to the saddle, but
there was no doubt of the final outcome. Hawke cringed, again
craning his neck in an attempt to get a better look at the rider,
while back in the camp another pair of men fought the horses
that were pulling at their picket pins, whinnying their fear.

Three. Three men. The number rang a bell of warning deep in
Hawke's unconscious even before he began to give the situation
careful thought. Then he got his first clear look at the rider
fighting his panicked mount just as the man was thrown clear of
the saddle, heading for a rock-hard landing.

It was one of the detectives the railroad had hired to track
them, one of the two Hawke had seen clearly at the last train
they had taken. For a moment Hawke stared in open disbelief as
Tom Fisher hit the ground with stunning force, his horse taking
to his heels at a high gallop.

Pronto and Ringo were muttering and swearing under their
breath, slowly picking themselves and their machines up out of
the dirt when Hawke gave the order.

"Start 'em up and let's ride!" he snapped, cutting through their
muttered oaths and accusations as to whose fault it had been,
hoping they would be able to start the machines. He had nothing
to go by, no gauge save themselves as to how much banging
around one of the machines could take before it simply refused
to start.

This time they were lucky. The motors roared back to life and
Hawke gave the signal to ride, but not before Tom Fisher, his
small green eyes narrowed and blazing, had gazed directly at
Hawke's black-attired figure astride the strange machine, recognition dawning in their depths, bitter anger riding across his
grim countenance.

CHAPTER 5

Hawke and his bunch had slammed their machines into high gear and were rolling out, heading for the tall timber, finishing the loop of the small hills when she appeared just like she had popped in out of thin air. Though they were not close enough to worry about the possibility of running into the light carriage, her horse jerked his head around in their direction and took off in a headlong run, bit clamped between its teeth.

Swearing bitterly under his breath, Hawke signaled his men away from the panicked beast. The closer they got to the animal the worse it would get. There was nothing they could do. If, while on their motorcycles they tried to stop the horse, matters would quickly deteriorate from worse to impossible. The young woman in the carriage, thank God, at least seemed to know how to handle a horse. The animal was a runaway, but she had not lost the reins in the first startling moments, and she was half standing in the carriage, like a chariot driver. Had Hawke seen the pasty white look of stark terror impressed across her fine features, he would not have been so confident of the outcome of their unexpected meeting. Nor would he have appreciated the momentary flash of recognition that had lit her brown eyes the first instant she had clamped eyes on him as he and the others had swept noisily around the base of the hills headed straight for her.

Had he seen the woman's face clearly, Hawke would have been converted to a firm believer in Fate, but he did not. He was aware only of the trim figure braced half upright against the carriage seat, the wind whipping the material of her dress around soft curves and long, slender legs. Long, shining blue-black hair was whipped out behind her in an unbridled cascade. And be-

yond her, coming down out of the hills, was Rawlins. Hawke
had not thought he would have to capitulate so soon, or so thoroughly, but for the moment, he was damn glad Rawlins was on a
horse instead of one of the motorcycles. Hawke relaxed. Rawlins
was going after the woman's terrified horse, and he had a way
with animals.

A glance over Hawke's shoulder told him all he needed to
know. The three detectives he had recognized were mounted and
hot on their trail. How they had caught the one horse the motorcycles had startled so quickly was a mystery, but still a fact.
They were pounding after them at a dead run. Grimly Hawke
smiled his satisfaction. This would be the first test of the superiority of the motorcycles. Horses would not be able to maintain
the top speed set by the machines. The Indians would not tire,
falter, or stick a hoof unexpectedly into a hole and throw one of
their riders. With another glance over his shoulder, Hawke sat
down to do some serious riding.

Salvador Hawke led, his men followed. The motorcycles were
still going strong, weaving through the trees, but the three in
pursuit were no longer visible. Not visible, but still there nonetheless. Not one of the detectives had chosen to go after
Rawlins, probably believing him to be the young lady's escort.
All three were hanging onto them as if they were stickers in a
horse's tail. Hawke planned on a sweep through Horse Thief
meadows to shed their pursuers before swinging back in the
direction of their secluded boxed valley. But there was one
problem. They were not losing them. The three were coming on
with dogged determination.

Topping out on the crest of a bald hill, Hawke signaled a stop
and Jackson minutely examined their back trail. There, far in
the distance, on the flat mesa miles behind, were three specks
that were the railroad detectives. It did not seem likely they were
going to give up easily.

"They're still coming," Jackson announced to no one in particular as they sat their machines atop the hill, the motors at
low idle, making talking a little easier. "They're still coming,"
Jackson repeated, "and there ain't no way to cover these damn

things' tracks." His tone made it undeniably plain that he was not happy with the situation as it stood.

"But we still have the advantage of speed," Hawke reminded him as well as the others.

"Not where everybody keeps falling off," Ringo put in, absently rubbing unmentionable sore spots.

"Feels like my innards are gonna bust," Pronto put in. There was nothing smooth or continental about the coarse comment.

"We knew when we started this that things might not exactly go smoothly in the beginning," Hawke pointed out stiffly, his voice holding the ring of authority, the sting of a leader being questioned. "Bugs always have to be worked out of something like this when you're the first to try it."

"We better be rid of these here bugs in a hurry," Pronto dug at Hawke, "they're hangin' on us like bluebottle flies in the summer."

Where the hell had those men come from? Hawke was silent, his lips compressed in a grim line, but the question preyed on his mind. How had they managed to find them, and so quickly? Hawke knew his bunch still needed time to work with the new motorcycles, and that time had just been snatched away from them. The railroad detectives were behind them, and the secret of their new machines was a secret no longer. As soon as they hit a town the three working for the railroad would put out the word on their change in mounts. They had to hit a train before that happened, Hawke decided. They had to have that element of surprise at least once. And until Jackson came up with a way to cover their tracks, or at least make them less obvious, they would have to depend on speed to keep them ahead of pursuers. That meant they would have to circle back to their hideout, collect Rawlins and their supplies, and abandon it. Without a doubt, it was time to move on.

"Well?" Pronto prodded. "You got any ideas?" Pronto loved the machines, but this was a fix not expected.

Hawke shot Pronto a sour look. In fact, he did have an idea, but he had a feeling none of them were going to like it. Well, he did not give a damn whether they liked it or not. He did not like it either, but it was better than anything he had heard Jackson come up with yet, which was exactly nothing.

"There's a creek up ahead," Hawke gunned his motor and took off without further explanation, the others strung out behind him,

As far as Hawke was concerned the Sangre de Cristos were a hospitable bunch of mountains. They had just about everything a man could ask for, depending, of course, on where he was at. There were streams, trees, steep slopes, and gentle grades. To the west and south were mesas and open flats. To the east of the vast expanse of mountains, the same. Hawke knew where he was, and what he needed was not far distant. They had been climbing steadily since their unexpected encounter with the power of the railroad, and that would be putting an extra burden on the horses as well. As the trail got steeper and the air thinner the animals would be blowing, if they were not in bad shape already.

Hawke slowed their pace as they entered the sheltering canopy of the pines. Beneath their wheels a soft spring carpet of pine needles appeared, and the deep, rutlike tracks they had been leaving in the dirt disappeared. As long as they kept the pace slow and did not pull any abrupt starts or stops that might dig up the carpet of brown needles, their passages would be nearly undetectable.

Glancing back behind him to observe the condition of the earth in their wake, Hawke grinned and motioned for Jackson to look back. Jackson's hard, angular face softened and broke into a familiar good-humored grin. It was the same logic they would follow for losing a horse's trail. Find some kind of country where hoofprints would be undetectable. They needed country where tire tracks would be unnoticeable. Not an easy order, but not impossible either. The main problem was noise. Motorcycles could be heard for miles around, the sounds of their engines bouncing off hillsides and echoing down canyons. That was an angle that would take some working on, but for the moment, this would have to do.

The stream Hawke had mentioned appeared, glittering

through the trees. He led the way to it, and into its rushing current. There was a place along the soft bank where a good tracker would be able to find where they had entered, but it would be the same for a horse. The machines just took a little getting used to, a little understanding. Hawke curbed an impulse to reach out and pat the thing's front carriage much as he would pat a horse's neck for a good performance. After all, this was a machine, and it did not need encouragement as a horse did.

On either side of them water sprayed up in tiny arched waterfalls, sending wide-spreading ripples to either bank. Large rocks split through the stream's surface, which sent the water cascading around them in a frothy tide. Deftly Hawke steered a course around the slippery rocks, Pronto, Ringo, and Hart Jackson following suit without difficulty.

Hawke left the stream at a steep slope where the aspen marched almost down to the water's edge. Limbs and trunks, now devoid of leaves in preparation for winter, shivered and quaked in the stirring of the chilled air. The bite of cold wind whipped up by the speed of the motorcycles reminded Hawke that he and his men would need warmer clothing. Hunching forward against the wind, he turned his cycle out of the creek upslope. There was a need too, he realized, to convert the saddle boots for their rifles so they could use them while astride their vehicles.

His thoughts fixed to the future, making plans and starting to work on some knotty problems. Hawke had not spared one for the novice riders coming up behind him. Hawke took the slope slick as butter in a hot pan. Jackson came up behind him with a little less grace, and Pronto followed with a showy flourish that went totally unobserved by the others.

Ringo followed, taking his cue from Pronto, felt the tires bite into the earth and take hold, felt the machine beneath him surge forward as he applied the gas with a growing confidence, felt the exhilaration of power surge through him just before the machine started going out from under him. His only recently won confidence crumbled and Ringo yowled and once again parted company with the motorcycle seat.

His starkly white hair flashing in the brilliant sun, Ringo rolled end over end in the direction gravity dictated. An exposed root jarred him rudely off course, but did not arrest his progress as he splashed into the creek, winding up flat on his back in the icy water staring up at the sky through the tangle of tree branches overhead. The motorcycle, riderless, fell over sideways, gouging itself into the earth and falling well short of the water.

At the top of the slope Hawke paused as Ringo's yowl pierced even the low growls of the combined motors. Catching sight of Ringo in the sparkling waters below, Hawke slapped one hand over his face in exasperation and gazed at Ringo through a couple of spread fingers. Never would he have believed it possible for one man to fall off so many times.

"Damn it!" Ringo swore, "how many times a man have to gentle one of these critters before it stays gentled?"

Limping a little, Ringo, dripping and shivering, gamely made his way back to his fallen mount, and huffing and puffing, pushed it to the top of the slope before attempting to start it again. With very little effort the thing roared back to life. Hawke silently thanked Mr. Hedstrom, the machine's originator, for the dependability so far, of his Indian motorcycle.

The sight of Ringo, wet, dripping, and covered with silt from the creek bottom gave Hawke pause to reconsider what he had in mind, but what he planned was not *that* dangerous. He had done something similar a number of times when he had been practicing. It was an escape route made for them. An offering from mother mountain herself, a place where it was highly unlikely the horses would follow. It would give them the lead they needed to circle back to the hideout, collect their supplies, and get clear out of the territory before the railroad detectives had a chance to figure out what was going on. It was, Hawke decided, genius. But then, there was Ringo.

Rawlins had had to push his mount hard to catch up with the runaway, but his horse had been fresh, and it had been plain for him to see that the horse had already covered several miles. Panic was always a strong driving force, and that animal had really panicked at the sight and sound of the speeding motorcycles. Surprisingly, the woman had managed to hang onto the reins, but the horse was still running strong, throwing off a foamy sweat and driving against the bit when Rawlins finally came up alongside.

With the motorcycles disappearing into small dots on the horizon, the sounds of their motors dimming to a low hum, and the three riders from the other side of the hills hot after them, paying no attention to Rawlins and the lady, it was not hard for him to ease the horse up and bring it to a snorting, disgruntled stop. Rawlins did not know what had happened around the other side of the hills, but whatever it was, he hoped Hawke would not be having too much trouble with the men who had taken out after them. Well, they were on their machines, and he on his horse. As far as Rawlins could see, all he could do was wait. In the meantime, there was the lady.

Releasing her calmed but blowing horse, Rawlins turned to her with a crooked smile on his lips, a twinkle in his eye, and tipped his hat.

"Name's Rawlins, ma'am," he told her, drinking in her beauty. "You all right?"

She looked like something Hawke might come up with. Lips, full and red, wearing a bonnet to protect her fair skin, hair the color of a raven's wing streaming out from underneath, and eyes, large and tilted like a cat's, regarded him from beneath a sweep of lash. When she smiled, it was first coy, then brilliant, beaming a dazzling set of straight, white teeth.

"I'm Erin Keller," she replied to Rawlins' unasked question in a low, purring voice. "And I'm just fine. I would have gotten things back under control shortly, but I am grateful for your intercession."

For a moment Rawlins looked blank.

"Your help," Erin clarified matters. "I'm grateful for it." Rawlins would have enjoyed sitting there and hearing her talk. Her voice, smooth as silk, was soft, almost caressing.

Shifting a bit in the saddle causing the leather to creak softly, he cleared his throat. His tall, rawboned frame made him seem to be wrapped around the horse he rode, and his brown eyes were alight with genuine concern.

"If you don't mind my sayin' so, ma'am," Rawlins began earnestly, "this here is still mighty dangerous country for a woman like you to be wanderin' around alone in."

Erin graced Rawlins with another of her bright smiles. "I'm all right, really." She paused as if not quite sure what to tell him, her composure slipping the slightest bit. "My father holds a post of some importance with the railroad. I'm going on a little farther to where I'll meet him."

"Well that helps some, but there ain't many in these parts who'd stop to ask you about such as who your pa is."

"I'll manage just fine," Erin returned evasively.

"I'd be glad to ride along with you for a spell," Rawlins offered in his slow, studied tones.

"No!" Erin blurted, then regained her poise, her hands fluttering to hold the reins loosely in her lap. "No, Mr. Rawlins," she said silkily, "I thank you for your kind offer, but I'll be quite all right." Her firm tone made it absolutely clear that she did not want him trailing along with her.

With a flash of a smile, Erin lifted the reins and snapped them smartly over the carriage horse's back, sending him off again at a sedate walk. She had recognized Rawlins from the day when she had been riding on the train and it had been robbed. He had been there, along with the other men who had been riding the strange machines. She had not lied about her father, unless it was to underestimate his importance. He owned what seemed like half the railroads in the country. She smiled to herself as she remembered the robbery she had witnessed. The thieves had even managed to take off with the engine in spite of the detectives on board the train. Such men as those four were her father's problem, and most certainly were not hers. In fact, the way things had been going lately between herself and her father, Erin Keller did not even want to hear about his problems ever again.

Concern was written in the lines of Rawlins' face as he watched the trim line of Erin's gray traveling dress move and sway in rhythm with the retreating carriage. The runaway horse had not appeared to upset her much. There had to be another kind of bee up her petticoats for her to take on so. Still, he was not about to press the issue. He had offered his help. She had refused. That was all there was to it. Rawlins glanced toward the snowcapped mountain peaks towering in the distance beyond the carriage, roughly in the same direction Hawke and the boys had taken. He could picture the mountains, the canyons, meadows, and basins in the distance, calculating which direction Hawke might have taken to cut back to their hideout, because return he would, for the supplies and the extra Indian.

Peering into the distance as if he could see through the towers of earth and rock that were the mountains, Rawlins grinned. He knew the perfect route for Hawke to circle back. Horse Thief meadow. Rawlins wheeled his horse to start out in the direction of the route's back door, but suddenly pulled himself up short. They could not come back that way. Hawke knew about the place, where heavy rains had torn out the trail above the canyon outside the approach. On horseback they had been forced to double back or risk losing the horses, and they had lost a good day of travel. Hawke could not come back that way.

The Indian throbbing its mechanical power beneath him, Salvador Hawke paused above the canyon trail, aiming a measuring gaze in the direction of the missing piece of trail. He had remembered the spot well, and the distance was no greater than his memory had supplied. It was an easy jump, one tailored to their needs. One even a total amateur could take with ease. Pronto had taken a couple of creek crossings and round-topped a couple of hills since his tumble by the creek in the valley. Hart Jackson was a solid rider, moving with the machine already as if he had grown to be a part of it, sailing above unexpected crests and drops as well as Hawke. But then, there was Ringo.

"What the devil we doin' up heres anyway?" Ringo demanded as they pulled up in a line confronting the drop that sliced away from their front wheels with the suddenness of the Grand Canyon's drop. As far as Ringo was concerned, the water-torn gorge could have been the Grand Canyon. Ringo's peculiar cool gray eyes were suspicious as they fastened themselves on Hawke.

Hawke was not quite sure about Ringo, but they had come this far, and as far as Hawke was concerned, turning back was out of the question. "We're going to jump it," Hawke informed him.

Pronto let out a wild war whoop, his black eyes flashing, and he reached to the handlebars to gun the engine in anticipation.

"Now let's just hold on here a minute," Ringo protested, his usually smooth round face deeply lined and troubled. He knew the answer to his next question, but felt compelled to ask it anyway. "How?"

"On these," Hawke patted his motorcycle almost lovingly. "This is what's going to keep us one step ahead of the law from now on."

"Sweet Jesus," Ringo swore barely above a whisper.

"Let's go!" Pronto urged, his face animated, his hands gripping the handlebars with a strength that turned his knuckles white.

"You can double back, take another trail around," Hawke reminded Ringo, not certain whether he wanted him to do it or not. Ringo knew the same as they that any other trail would take him perilously close to their pursuers, and the growl of the motorcycle was not likely to go undetected.

Ringo straightened a bit where he sat the motorcycle, the tip of his tongue coming out to moisten his lips.

"It's an easy jump." Hawke tried to sound offhanded about the matter. "You've already done it, more than once, on the way here, but there wasn't an open chasm to think about. It's a downhill drop from here to the other side. Couldn't be easier. I'll show you."

Turning his motorcycle, Hawke swung in a broad arch back in the direction they had come to start his run. As all eyes fastened on him he paused, gunned the Indian's engine a couple of times, hoping to impress Ringo with the power he possessed on top of one of those things, then roared forward as Pronto whipped up behind him from where he had started and kicked off hot on his heels.

The engines raced as the wheels left off contact with the ground and machine and rider rocketed out over the yawning abyss, first one rider, then the other, both airborne for a frozen instant in time as they arched one nearly directly behind the other and descended toward the ground on the far side, rear wheels touching the ground first, a good fifteen feet beyond the edge of the cut. It was precision, almost as if they had practiced the same jump together hundreds of times in the past.

Jackson shrugged and put out a foot to balance himself as he turned his machine and started to follow suit. Ringo gulped in an unwanted stomachful of air and after a brief moment of indecision, turned his motorcycle, hurrying after Hart Jackson. Ringo had no choice but to try, and if he was going to try, he was determined he would not try it alone.

The wind rippled through Hart Jackson's close-cropped black hair as he started his machine forward, lifting it almost immediately to a high speed for the jump. Alongside, Ringo jumped his motorcycle ahead only a heartbeat after Jackson. The run was short, then instantly the land fell away from beneath his wheels, and Ringo felt his heart leap into his throat. Only dimly was he aware of Jackson's cycle racing along with his own, but nothing could distract him from the yawning emptiness that had opened up beneath him.

Then they were coming down. It was as if a giant hand had cradled their flight across the interminable space and was about to deposit them again safely upon the face of mother earth. Ringo felt an electric excitement race through him such as he had never felt before as first one, then the other wheel touched down well clear of the edge. Sweat beading his forehead in a shimmering veil and his eyes glazed, Ringo brought his machine to a halt alongside Hawke's and turned his head to gaze back over his shoulder at the open crevice with an unconcealed awe.

CHAPTER 6

It was dusk, the moon rising up out of the east like a giant silver orb, hanging low in the sky, still brushing the treetops in the far mountains when Rawlins detected the first distant hum of the approaching motorcycles. At the corral the horses heard it as well, growing louder by the second. The sound, one they had decided not to like from the very first time it had been heard in the once-peaceful valley, started a sort of nervous snorting and shuffling among them as the growling, oncoming roar of the engines increased in volume.

Rawlins walked to the corral and stepped inside to quiet the animals as the machines swept up to the shack one after another, lining up in front of the hitching post just like they belonged there while the horses whinnied, tossed their heads, and with a rush started for the far side of the corral. As the horses whipped past him, hoofs pounding the hard earth, Rawlins jumped for the corral crossbars. He started to swear loudly, his words echoing across the valley as one by one the motorcycles were shut off, but the horses were not quieted nearly so easily.

Though he was tired and trail-worn, the success of the day warmed Hawke's humor as he strolled in the direction of the corral where Rawlins still attempted to reason with the animals, talking to them as if they were a collection of old friends.

"Got your hands full?" Hawke called across the quickly gathering darkness. "Feels good," he prodded, "to climb down off what got you from here to there and forget about it." His meaning was clear, but Rawlins did not rise to the bait. Before going on Hawke paused a long minute. "There's still a lone Indian on that hill over there," he nodded in the direction of the hill where they had launched their day's expedition.

The noise and quick movement eliminated with the shutdown of the mortorcycles, the horses were quieting, calming into a milling mass of horseflesh, covering the length of the corral and back again repeatedly in a matched, choppy trot.

Rawlins gave Hawke a slow smile, the edges of his lips curling up as he looked from Hawke to the lone motorcycle still occupying a spot on the low hill Hawke had indicated, then looked at Hawke again. Rawlins sighed, taking a long, deep breath, and paused as if he were about to speak the wisdom of the ages.

"Reckon I'll just stick with the horses," he said evenly, then jumped lightly over the top corral post and walked slowly back to the shack.

If Hawke had been forced to admit it, he was not really surprised. Still, there was no time for slow convincing. They were going to have to pull out of there with the sunrise, a fact Rawlins was well aware of as evidenced by the gear that lay packed and ready on the rickety porch. Their maneuver at the chasm had bought a couple days of valuable time—time they could not waste waiting for Rawlins to be trailing alone behind them with the horses. If they wanted surprise on their side they were going to have to hit a train, and hit it soon, before the three detectives had a chance to spread word of their new method of operation. Hawke was completely aware of the assets their motorcycles possessed. They had speed, maneuverability and, for the moment, surprise. But they had to take advantage of it now. The first time out they would need all the advantages they could line up.

Glancing up at the unbelievably clear night sky, Hawke paused where he stood, never ceasing to marvel at the clarity of the mountain skies. His eyes swept past the dazzling silver glow of the newly rising moon, reaching higher in the blackness among the shimmering lights that lit the night sky. Then he saw it. One of the larger spots of light seemed to detach itself from its proper place among its fellows and plummeted across the sky in a trailing arch. At the same instant he felt a cold shiver run up his spine as if someone had stepped on his grave. Hawke frowned. If he believed in omens, this had to be one. He was glad he did not believe in them.

Turning, Hawke stomped off after Rawlins. That man needed some serious talking to and convincing, and he needed it tonight. Hawke did not like to think about leaving Rawlins behind, not to mention the extra Indian motorcycle parked on the hill above the shack, but leave him he would if it came to that. Hawke had not expected this abrupt need to pull out so soon after the men had tried out their new transportation, but that was in part why he had come up with the Indian idea in the first place. The ability to more easily rise to the unexpected. To move faster, as the rest of the world seemed to be doing already. He had hoped to have more time to convince Rawlins through demonstration and action, but it appeared the weight of his words was going to be the only weapon he had. Perhaps what Rawlins had witnessed from the hills earlier that day would help to sway him. Hawke did not know, but he had to try.

It was about then that Hawke remembered the girl and the runaway carriage. He paused in midstride, pondering. Who was she? Where the devil had she come from and where had she been going anyway out there in the middle of nowhere, alone? He had been too far distant to get a clear look at her, but something in her trim form, something about the way she had held herself had telegraphed to Hawke that she had been a beauty. Undoubtedly Rawlins had the answers, but he did not seem overly eager to impart them. Then Hawke smiled. He had not given the man much of a chance. Maybe later, after he convinced him about the motorcycles.

Hawke lifted the door latch and his thoughts jerked back to their immediate problem. It had really raised his temper to spot those three out there today. They were an added problem he had not counted on. They were persistent, he had to give them that much. Somehow they had managed to nearly track them down, and Hawke did not much care for that fact. No real threat as Hawke saw it, but they were a petty annoyance that was not likely to go away in the immediate future. He sighed and entered the shack, his boots thudding hollowly on the aging wood floor. Later, after they had taken a few trains, he planned on leading those three railroad men on a wild-goose chase that would run their horses right into the ground. For now though that would have to wait. Tom Fisher, Will Barnett, and Sam West were hardly more than names Hawke had but recently attached to faces, and while he was aware of their abilities, he was equally well aware of his own. The hiring of them would make no more difference to the road than any one of a hundred other attempts they had made to trap Salvador Hawke and his gang on other occasions.

Anticipating the return of the others, Rawlins had thoughtfully put on some grub. The shack was filled with the smell of warming beans, sizzling bacon, and boiling coffee. Pronto was tending it, stirring the beans occasionally, poking the bacon and keeping an eye on the bubbling coffee while Rawlins leaned back in a not-too-steady chair, feet up, a bemused expression on his long face while he listened to Ringo's ardent words of praise for the motorcycles and the genius who thought up the idea in the first place, Hawke. With all the fervor of a convert, he attacked Rawlins' hesitancy to try the new machine.

"If you'd 'a been on horses, movin' quiet and Jackson here lookin' for sign, you wouldn't'a run into them three thataway in the first place," Rawlins pointed out when Ringo had finished his dissertation of their great escape.

Ringo brushed his objection aside. "They were out there, and they were trackin' us. They would'a found us one way or another. We drew them off you, Rawlins. One look at us and they weren't interested in you no more."

Rawlins nodded in slow agreement. "That's why I wasn't chased halfway to Colorado and back. Don't like machines."

"We're pulling out in the morning, Rawlins," Hawke reminded him, "and we're pulling out on those machines. Just what are you aimin' to do? You won't be able to keep up, and we won't be able to hang back for you."

Picking up a tin plate and a cup, Rawlins headed for the pot of beans and dinner. "Me and the horses'll be along. Might even bring the wagon and haul that extra thing of yours down for you."

Hawke threw up his hands in disgust. "In just three days we're going to be near Auton Chico, and we're going to take that train."

Squatting by the fire, Rawlins took a forkful of food and began chewing slowly, appearing to gaze off into space. "Tell ya' what," he said, brown eyes alight with humor. "If I ain't there you all can take the train without me. But don't worry none about it 'cause I'll be there."

"Even if you get there by then," Hawke pushed him, "how will you keep up when we ride out? A horse just can't keep up with those machines," Hawke protested, trying hard to make the man see reason. "They don't have to rest, they don't have to eat or drink."

"I'll just tag along," Rawlins interrupted Hawke's protests. "If I don't manage to catch up with you, you can split my share of the take."

"You're going to get yourself hanged," Hawke protested. "If they send some kind of posse out after us and find only you in our dust what do you think will happen?"

Rawlins chuckled. "With you fellas on those contraptions makin' all that noise you figure they're gonna take out after me?" He shook his head in patient disbelief.

"You saw how fast those contraptions can move today," Hawke reminded him. "You were watching from the hills. They aren't going to have a chance of catching up with us, and that'll leave you."

"I wasn't sure myself, in the beginning," Ringo put in stoutly, "but I am now. Why, Hawke bought us two days' time, and here we don't even know what we're doin' yet. Why, you give those machines half a chance and they'll change a whole way of livin'."

"Don't want my way of livin' changed," Rawlins maintained. "I like horses. Don't like machines," he repeated. "Now, I took care of myself just fine before I met up with you boys years back, and I can do the same now. 'Sides, we'll still be workin' together, just won't see as much of each other as before. Leastways that's the way it appears." He paused, thoroughly chewing a mouthful of food, as if that fact were indeed in doubt, and swallowed. Then he went on. "Ain't nothin'," he said plainly, leaving no more room for argument or persuasion, "goin' to get me on one of them things."

Those were Rawlins' last words on the subject. With the coming of dawn, the sun barely a phantom to light the tops of the distant trees with an approaching glow, Hawke, Ringo, Hart Jackson, and Pronto were lined up outside the shack, mounted on the Indians and ready to pull out. Bedrolls and supplies were tied on the backs of machine saddles, and rifle scabbards had been mounted much as they had been on horse saddles, muzzles slung toward the ground, stocks braced beneath handlebars. There was a bite to the early-morning mountain air, and Hawke was glad it had not snowed during the night.

Some distance off, Rawlins was packed up and ready to go as well. He had the wagon loaded lightly, carrying only a few supplies, and perversely, the fifth Indian. The horses were all tied on behind and the machine had been carefully covered with an old blanket to shield it from the eyes of the skittish animals.

Hawke tried to conceal his irritation, but it was a difficult task. It would have been bad enough, Rawlins attempting to accompany them on horseback, but with the wagon . . . The whole thing was starting to get under his skin, as he knew Rawlins intended it to. The man thought the whole idea of machines traveling independently over the earth as idiotic and impossible, and he was needling them because of it. But Hawke had faith in the Indian motorcycles. At the same time he feared he was going to lose a good man in Rawlins because his negative expectations where the motorcycles were concerned were going to backfire in his face. Hawke hoped he would have the good sense to cut and run when the facts became as apparent to Rawlins as they were to him. He hated to think of Rawlins ending up in some prison or getting himself hanged because of his stupid stubbornness.

Nodding to the others, Hawke kicked his machine into life, hearing one after the other join him in the now-familiar growling purr that was the cycles at rest. At the abrupt eruption of the din, Rawlins had his hands full with the pair of horses that drew the wagon. They rolled their eyes until the whites showed, and half rose in the harnesses, nearly jerking the reins from his upheld hands. To the rear, the horses tied on behind whinnied their fear, tugging at the securely tied lead ropes that held them fast.

With one last look behind him, Hawke turned the machine and put it to the trail, Jackson, Ringo, and Pronto stringing out behind him in an at least momentarily evenly spaced line. Pride swelled within Hawke and he put his thoughts to what lay ahead: Auton Chico and their first train in a new way of life.

This time the detectives would be far behind them. They would not be on hand to interfere. Their swift ride through the country the day before had bought them that much. Even stubborn Rawlins would have some extra time. The man was a good tracker, and had learned much from Jackson about covering trail, as had they all. They had carefully concealed what remained of the drums of fuel back at the shack in case they would have a reason to swing back that way again soon. Rawlins had insisted on carrying some on the wagon and some was stashed in other places, far scattered, where Hawke had left it for emergencies. And besides all the hidden fuel, Hawke knew of several places where he could get some more if needed.

Life, Hawke decided as they swept out of the protected valley and back into the wide-open world, was sweet after all. He had their destination and route already worked out in his mind. They would skirt the edge of the mountains, staying to the lower hills in consideration of their joint inexperience with the machines, swinging south and more to the east.

Where just the day before they had run into mounted detectives and a lovely lady gone astray, there was no one. Hawke knew the whereabouts of the three railroad men, or about where they would be, assuming they were backtracking to come after them. It was the woman he wondered about. Where the devil had she come from, and where had she gone? He regretted that he had not taken the opportunity to question Rawlins on the matter. Hawke had not been able to get a really good look at her, but even from a distance there had been something about the woman. Something almost magnetic. The feeling, odd though it was, that he had seen her somewhere before, not too long ago.

Hawke brought his motorcycle to a halt near the place where her carriage had taken off when their cycles had appeared around the base of the hills. He was sure he would be finding out more about her sooner or later. Gunning the motor, he was about to turn south when he saw it. Jackson saw it about the same time, bringing his vehicle up alongside Hawke's.

"Dust off to the north," Jackson commented above the idle of the engines. He squinted into the distance, his brown eyes sharp as any eagle's. "Looks like three riders," he added grimly, "and they ain't exactly takin' it easy." The meaning of his tone was clear. He figured them to be the same three riders they had lost in the canyons the day before.

"Can't be!" Ringo put in. "Why, we jumped that there gulch to lose them fellas."

Hawke frowned, squinting his blue eyes against the brilliant light that flooded across the mountains, lighting the dust that rose around the riders with a golden glow that was nearly impenetrable. Still, there was little doubt that Jackson was correct in his estimation. At least three riders were out there—Hawke had been able to discern that much through the golden, dusty haze. And it did not seem likely that it could be three different riders out here in the middle of nowhere in a big hurry to get somewhere.

Apparently the railroad detectives had come up with more sense than Hawke had been willing to give them credit for. They had not backtracked and circled to pick up their trail, as Hawke had anticipated. They had instead headed directly back for their starting point, probably anticipating the fact that Hawke and his bunch would be circling back toward home ground. They had undoubtedly ridden all night to be where they were now, coming down the trail. And by now there could be no doubt that they had heard the sound of the motorcycles in the hills above them.

Swearing eloquently, Hawke turned off the crest, his machine spewing dust and rocks from beneath spinning wheels. The detectives would have to rest their animals soon. This time Hawke was determined to put plenty of miles between himself and them. There was no way horses could keep up when the Indians were on the move. A smile twitched impatiently at the corners of Hawke's mouth. They had done it for Rawlins again. Those three would be drawn off in time for him to follow along behind in complete safety. It was very doubtful that the three might think of looking behind themselves for a stray fifth member of the gang hauling his motorcycle along in a wagon. Still, there was the more sober side to the situation. Hawke doubted that they would be seeing Rawlins again. Once they hit Auton Chico and the train, they would be moving fast, and Hawke could see no way Rawlins would be able to get that wagon there within the three days it would take the motorcycles to reach there. To Hawke's knowledge, it was not possible.

With a grim shake of his head, Hawke shifted his eyes straight forward. They had lost a good man in Rawlins. Progress, he decided, was going to extract a high price in payment.

George Rawlins topped the cut about the time Hart Jackson and Salvador Hawke had spotted the three riders coming down the pike after them. He also spotted the riders, but knew his own position was secure, well out of their line of vision through the scrub trees and piñon. His long legs braced in the wagon box, his brown eyes alight with an amused glint, Rawlins took in the unexpected scene that met his gaze. Evidently those detective boys had not been as easy to run around the bush as Hawke and the others had figured. Even so, they were not exactly in imminent danger of catching up with the roaring Indian motorcycles and their riders.

A slow smile sort of snuck up on him, wrapping itself around the oversized plug of tobacco Rawlins was chewing as he watched the strange parade pass before his eyes. He had to hand it to the detectives, they were stuck like burrs to saddle blankets, and the horses they were riding were mighty fine to have come this far so quick. But they were going to have to rest those animals mighty soon, and Hawke and the boys had just started out fresh with mechanical beasts that would need no resting. Rawlins had a feeling the situation was going to be interesting.

In an easy gesture, Rawlins lifted the reins and clucked to his horses. Heads up, ears pricked forward anxiously, they started forward at a spritely gait. Wagon wheels rumbled softly over hard ground, wood creaking in protest. The horses moved together, their hoofs making a pleasant, rhythmic sound against the earth they trod. Rawlins knew the trails in these parts better than most. He would follow along behind the procession for a piece, then take the cutoff and slide on down to Auton Chico. Cutting through the mountains instead of swinging around them would save him better than a day and a half's travel time. That would get him there well ahead of the persistent railroad men and in plenty of time to rejoin Hawke and the others to take the train out a short distance from there. After that, it was anybody's guess, but Rawlins had no intention of giving up his cut of what they would get from the holdup. So he was going to make it his business to stick with Hawke and the boys no matter what impressive feats the Indian manned machines were supposed to do. Rawlins never had put much stock in machines and he was sure he never would.

CHAPTER 7

Hart Jackson, scouting ahead astride his motorcycle as he had from horseback in the past, located an ideal spot for a camp in Blanco Canyon a few miles southwest of Auton Chico within easy striking distance of the train they were going to rob. All that remained for them to do was to make plans and wait for the train to come chugging down the tracks. The night before they had set up camp, and it was well over a day and a half before the train was due. The railroad detectives had been left in their first dust, and Jackson was devising new ways to help cover the tire tracks the motorcycles left in their wake. So far his success was marginal, but at least they were not leaving a clear trail right to their camp. Several times the tracks had been interrupted and altered by Jackson's ingenuity, although Hawke was not worried anyway. It was over three days to Auton Chico from their old hideout in the mountains on horseback. Fisher, Barnett, and West, the railroad men, could not possibly get this far until after they had already robbed the train and left in a cloud of dust.

Leaning back against a rock beneath the shade of a tree, Hawke gazed out across the narrow stream were the machines were parked. Traveling with them was a joy. There was no saddling or unsaddling to be done, no rubdowns to be given, no food or water to be sought out for their well-being. Best of all, there was no worry about picketing them securely to be sure they would still be where they had been left with the coming of the dawn. Hawke felt better than he had at any time he could remember in the last couple of years. This time things would come off without a hitch. He could feel it in his bones.

The day passed in lazy anticipation as Hawke alternately dozed beneath the shady tree or rose to wipe the collection of

dust from the still-new Indians. Hart Jackson, in his usual bois-
terous good humor, had ridden his motorcycle off to scout the
terrain surrounding the spot where they planned to stop the
train. Ringo was off on foot somewhere trying to scare up something for dinner to end their regime of hardtack and jerky, and
Pronto was occupying himself with the dynamite charges they
would be using to halt the train. Pronto worked like an artist,
lighting a couple of lengths of fuse attached to nothing to
recheck the timing and tying the proper-size charge for their
needs. As usual, they needed something impressive enough to
cause the engineer to slam on the brakes, but not so powerful as
to tear up the tracks. Even in the dim light of remembering the
last time they had gone out, a happening he really preferred to
forget, Hawke still wanted to avoid damage to the tracks. Actually he preferred to forget the entire occurrence save the fact
that it had been the last straw, the reason for procuring the Indians. Hawke realized that this time, being their first time out
with the motorcycles, things could get a bit tricky. Unpredicta-
ble elements were involved. They would have to be cautious in
this uncharted territory, but in return it would open up new
paths for them and give the railroads new problems to think
about.

While giving additional thought to the possibility of having
Pronto make up an extra charge to blow the old shack that stood
beside the tracks a little way outside Auton Chico, Hawke's
thoughts were scattered by the approaching buzz of Jackson's
machine. Hawke stood up, picking bits of dried grass from his
black jacket as Jackson came on, moving fast. When a man rode
like that there was no middle ground. Either it was good news or
it was bad, but it damn well had to be something to get excited
about. Hawke frowned as Jackson pulled up, killed the engine,
and joined them, dark face lit by the sparks that shot from his
brown eyes and the roguish grin that curled his lips.

"I spotted 'em," Jackson announced without preamble in the
ringing silence that fell in the wake of the engine's roar. "I spotted 'em coming up the trail. Knew just where we'd be, that ole
son!"

For an instant Hawke's mind went blank, then he caught sight of the wagon lumbering steadily up the trail that led down the canyon. Rawlins! It could not be. The man had not had time to cover half the distance pulling that wagon and leading all five horses.

But as the wagon drew closer, Pronto put down his work and joined Jackson and Hawke in staring. It was Rawlins, all right. The horses were moving with a light step, fresh as if they had just started out after a good feed and night's rest while Rawlins sat up attempting to whistle wetly around a wad of tobacco.

Eyes round with good humor and hands firm but gentle on the reins, Rawlins grinned as he splashed across the creek, "Howdy, boys," he said evenly, as if he had seen them only minutes before. "'Bout got things lined up?" He paused, looking from one face to another in the long silence. "Jackson's gettin' better hidin' the tracks of them things. I didn't find you near as easy as I expected."

"How . . ." Hawke began. "With the wagon it's not . . . I mean, even those detectives on horseback will take until late tomorrow or early the day after to get this far."

His long face serious, Rawlins stopped chewing for a moment, his gaze sweeping the three men who faced him. Then grinned again. "Shortcut."

"Shortcut?" Hawke demanded, stiff-lipped. "Rawlins, all these years we've been riding these trails, and you never said anything about a shortcut before." Hawke's figure in back cut an imposing presence, shoulders broad, filling out the expertly tailored jacket and flat-crowned black hat pulled low over narrowed blue eyes, hiding them in the shadow of the brim.

Climbing down from the wagon, Rawlins shrugged. "We ain't never needed it before, and you never asked me." He turned his head and spat tobacco juice in a long brown stream. "Be glad to show it to you boys next time through," he added agreeably as he stroked the neck of the horse nearest him.

Hawke did not bother to question Rawlins any closer. It was easy to see now why he had been so confident he would be able to catch up with them before they stopped the train near Auton

Chico. But Hawke was a bit surprised at the devious streak they had inadvertently uncovered in Rawlins. It gave a man pause to stop and wonder what other little tricks the man might have hidden up his sleeve that none of them had suspected before. Hawke turned from him as Ringo rode in with a rabbit for dinner, and Rawlins fell to unharnessing the horses. Then he turned back again.

"I don't reckon you caught sight of those railroad detectives anywhere along the way?" Hawke asked as an apprehensive afterthought.

Rawlins paused in what he was doing to turn to face Hawke squarely. Then Rawlins' long, thin face broke into an amused smile. "They didn't know the shortcut neither," he said with a mellow chuckle that bubbled through his mouthful of tobacco juice before he spit.

Feeling peculiarly at ease and optimistic about the following day's undertakings and the plans they had set, Hawke strolled over to start the fire for Ringo's rabbit stew. After all, Rawlins still had the fifth Indian in the back of the wagon. Maybe there was hope for him yet.

The following day dawned brilliantly, the sun warming from the moment it was spotted rising above the distant mountains. Salvador Hawke and his bunch had been up and moving since before the first sign of the sun. But, at its appearance, Hawke took it as a blessing of their undertaking. Rawlins had his horse singled out and saddled and the others were picketed stoutly a good distance away from where they would be starting up the machines. Rawlins' horse seemed to be the least skittish around the motorcycles, although Hawke did not know how the man hoped to handle the animal once they were moving, engines roaring, and wound up confronting a train to boot.

The animals Rawlins had brought, and he had brought along every last one of them, seemed almost haunted when Hawke chanced to shoot a glance in their direction. It was almost as if they both resented and feared the loud, clanging machines that had so obviously replaced them. Hawke pulled himself up short. That kind of thinking went better with George Rawlins. Hawke

was not about to soften in his resolve. The machines they straddled were the coming thing, and this day would prove his stance
beyond a doubt.

Rawlins led off, getting well clear of the immediate area as
one by one they kicked the growling machines into life, each
man now handling his machine like a veteran, talking to it,
coaxing and pushing it. They would cut a wide swing around
Rawlins on horseback and meet him near where they would set
the explosives.

As usual, Hawke had decided the simple method was the most
effective. They would set their charges near the tracks a good
way outside the town, set them off when the train approached,
bringing it to a hault, board it, and take the payroll money
Hawke knew it to be carrying. Then they would split up, reas-
semble some miles out, near the canyon where they had camped,
giving Rawlins a chance to get back to his horses and wagon and
head for the tall timber. And there was where Rawlins was sure
to fall well behind. Unless, of course, he knew some other shortcuts. That though was impossible. Nobody could know that
many shortcuts. Then he would find out how far behind the Indian motorcycles he would run. Oddly, Hawke hoped they
would not lose sight of him too soon. Toting that fifth Indian
around had to mean something. Maybe the reason was that he
sensed somehow that he would sooner or later come to his senses
and join them. Perhaps this train robbery was to be the testing
ground, the dry run that would convince Rawlins of his error in
not going along in the first place. Hawke pushed the hopeful
thoughts from his mind and rode. First, there was the train.

The train was already more than two hours late. That in itself
was not unusual in those parts, but this time Hawke did not heed
the added worry. The motorcycles were parked behind a low
bluff near the tracks. Pronto had expertly set the charges, bringing the fuses to Hawke. They were set to blow a good-sized crater on either side of the tracks and to take out the old leaning
shack about twenty yards northwest of their position. Rawlins
had tied his horse in the same general vicinity as the motorcycles. He and his horse seemed to have worked out a sort of ar-

rangement regarding the machines. Only once during their approach to the spot did the horse slew sideways beneath Rawlins, and that had been when Hawke and the others had roared past at a distance, taking the lead away from the easygoing, unhurried Rawlins.

Again Hawke took the gold watch from the pocket in his vest where it safely resided, buttoned in and attached to a gold chain. The hour was growing later by the minute, and still there was no sign of the train. The sun was glowing and warm overhead, already past its zenith. From this point on they would be losing daylight hours necessary to allow them to put many miles between themselves and any possible pursuit. Not that pursuers would have a chance in hell of catching up to them under any circumstances, even from a dead heat start, but Hawke was determined that this first time out things should go smoothly. He wanted plenty of margin for error, especially since Ringo was prone to making so many of them. Hawke swore under his breath as he swatted his black hat against his black-trousered leg in an attempt to shake loose the accumulating dust.

Pronto was pacing behind the bluff, wearing a path in the earth where he so earnestly strode. Rawlins, one who should be the most concerned with the delay, lay sprawled on his back curved to fit the hillside, hat pulled low over his eyes to block out the glaring sun and breathed in long, even breaths as if in slumber. Ringo just sat, checking and rechecking his pistol as he pulled it expertly from the holster. To make matters worse, Hawke had been alternately puffing on and allowing to burn out the cigars he so intensely disliked. It was a habit with him, lighting the fuses with the tip of a red-glowing cigar. A match would have done just as well, but old habits were hard to break.

Wordlessly, Hart Jackson strode out into the open alongside the railroad tracks. Sweeping his hat from his head, he knelt on the earth and laid an ear along the sun-warmed silver rail. After a time, he half rose, drawing his bowie knife from his belt and stabbed it into the earth, gingerly laying an ear alongside the hilt, then withdrawing it partially, laid light, almost caressing fingers along the expanse of exposed blade. With a satisfied grunt, he stood up and strode back behind the bluff where Hawke was waiting expectantly.

"It's coming," Jackson said flatly.

Hawke strained his eyes, gazing down the track for some distant sign of the engine. He was almost sure Jackson was losing his grip when far in the distance, appearing almost as if it were a mirage, the train loomed into sight.

Once again relighting the cigar clenched between his teeth, Hawke caused the tip to glow red. A light appeared in the depths of his blue eyes as they narrowed against the curling gray smoke. The train came on. They were ready, by God, Hawke grinned, they were ready. Like an old mottled snake the train twisted its way up the tracks headed right for their trap. Hawke watched it come on, gauging its speed, hesitating another instant before touching the glowing tip of the cigar to the cluster of three fuses Pronto had earlier placed in his hand.

At the touch of the cigar, all three fuses leaped to life, a sparking flame speeding down their lengths, racing the train for that spot along the track. Hawke's practiced eye told him it's going to come out right. The fuses were timed just right. The dynamite would blow in plenty of time for the engineer to throw on the brake and slide to a stop before the spot where the dynamite tore up the earth.

They were ready. They had prepared for this, and they were ready. There was no doubt in Hawke's mind about that. The fatigue of the past hours of waiting fell away from him like a cloak from his shoulders. For once it would be easy. His only regret was that he would not be able to see the looks on the faces of the people when he and his men remounted their motorcycles and thundered off into the hills.

The train was coming, its even chugging and rhythmic clatter over the rails music to Hawke's ears as the fuses burned to their source and a booming explosion that made the earth shudder ripped into his concert. Dust was rising in a thick cloud as in a mere instant the half-tumbled shack followed suit, wood flying wildly in ever direction, dirt clods and pebbles beginning to rain earthward at the termination of their flight as the engine plowed full steam into the middle of the havoc wreaked by the explosives. Hawke gawked in surprise. The damn fool was not slowing! What was he trying to do? Get every passenger on board killed? The damn fool was risking everything on the assumption that behind the thick curtain of dust and debris the dynamite had not taken out the tracks into a broken, bent tangle of metal and splintered wood.

Bellowing like a maddened bull, Hawke swore wildly as he headed for the parked motorcycles. Rawlins had beat him there, and was mounted on his horse and riding hard after the train that had slowed slightly, and was now hurrying down the tracks, leaving its attackers behind like a dragon unperturbed by the pinprick of a knight's lance.

The hoofs of George Rawlins' horse were pounding hard, digging deep into soft earth as he plunged headlong, unthinkingly after the slowed but still moving train. His horse was game, leaning into the bit, striving stride for stride to reach the back of the train and pull up alongside it.

Suddenly, behind him, a new sound ripped through the cool, crisp air. Hawke and the others had reached the motorcycles and brought them to life. The horse's ears flicked forward, then back, reaching for the alien sound he so disliked.

Like a pack of screaming Indians, for which they had been named, the motorcycles came off the hill in hot pursuit of the unco-operative train. Dust and pebbles flew from beneath spinning tires, and the familiar deep growl of the pack of engines assailed Rawlins' ears as well as those of his running horse. Expecting the animal to shy, Rawlins prepared himself as the machines roared up behind them, splitting around them and whipping past in a wild dash for the money. But instead of panicking, Rawlins' horse seemed almost to pick up the challenge of a race the machines and their riders, sitting so close to the earth, offered, and started to fly along in their wake even faster.

The train's last car slipped by, then another. He had caught it! Hawke could have thrown back his head and laughed in the wind at the futility of the train's attempted escape from them now that they too were equipped with fast-moving machines.

Jackson, Ringo, and Pronto fanned out around and to either side of him, grim looks that seemed to go with riding the Indians etched deeply into their faces. Hawke was conscious of the same lines deep in his own face in spite of the urge he had to laugh. The only difference was the slight quirk of his lips at the corner, and anyone seeing it would have sworn he had been touched by the devil.

Hawke spotted the baggage car then, the car that would be carrying the cash they were after. He pressed his machine forward, the others with him following suit and chanced to glance up at that moment. There, precariously balanced on the roof of one of the cars poised to jump to the next atop the swift-moving train was George Rawlins. His horse behind them, abandoned and riderless, was falling farther behind by the second.

With renewed determination, Hawke spurted his machine forward, drawing up alongside the baggage car with ease. Then, in spite of the fact that he was riding much lower now than when he had been astride a horse, Hawke managed to reach up with one hand while still guiding his cycle with the other and throw the baggage door open. A startled young man, thin and bespectacled, jumped up from where he had been bending over, apparently sorting mail, and stared out at them in disbelief. Never had he seen such a sight as the four men astride the strange machines, keeping pace with the train with apparent ease. The added sight of Pronto riding abreast and a little ahead of Hawke, holding his gun pointed shakily in the young man's direction, did nothing to bring surcease as Rawlins placed sun-browned knobby hands firmly in position and somersaulted into the car as it continued to rattle down the tracks. Catlike, Rawlins managed to land on his feet inside the swaying car as the wheel clackety-clacked over the rails in a rhythm that seemed to be picking up speed.

Hawke knew they either had to stop the train or move fast. Whether or not the engineer up front was aware of anything, Hawke could not be sure. The noise up front created by the laboring engine could have drowned out the noise the motorcycles were making in keeping pace with the last section of the speeding train. The thought brought a faint smile to Hawke's wind-pinched face. If they could pull this off, the engineer might not even be aware a robbery had taken place until they reached the next town. Unless Hawke missed his guess, the man in the baggage car was not the sort to risk climbing over the tops of the cars to inform the engineer of something that could no longer be prevented or changed.

Gritting his teeth until his jaw muscles twitched, Hawke reached for the bar to swing aboard, conscious of the motorcycle purring beneath him and not quite sure how he was going to pull it off. With a lurch and a twist, Hawke jerked himself aboard the speeding car, managing to keep his legs clear of the spot where the wheels met the tracks with sheering knifelike precision as his motorcycle roared off without him and took an unguided nose dive into the dust. At least it had not careened beneath the wheels, and for the moment, Hawke could only hope that it had not been damaged, seriously or otherwise.

Rawlins had drawn his gun and shifted his tall, rawboned frame into a menacing stance, his long brown hair whipped wild by the wind, his brown eyes twin pools of calm as Hawke regained his dignity after clambering aboard.

"The payroll!" Hawke barked, "and be quick about it!"

Out of the corner of his eyes, Hawke could see Pronto starting to move his motorcycle forward, inching along the side of the train with the obvious intent of reaching the engine and forcing the engineer to stop. Jackson stayed alongside, dividing his attention between keeping his Indian from throwing him unexpectedly and holding his gun on the car's interior. Ringo stuck by him, both hands firmly planted on the hand grips, his gaze fixed straight ahead, save for occasional glances to the side to see how things were progressing.

"Nnnnno payroll on this train," the clerk stammered.

"No payroll!" Hawke bellowed, pressing his face almost into the clerk's. "Don't try to con me, boy," he warned him, an edge to his voice, his eyes narrowing with anger, his mustache twitching with the frustration that tore at him. "I don't have time. I know damn well there's a payroll on this train and I aim to have it!"

The young clerk's head bobbed up and down rapidly in agreement. "Yes, sir, there was supposed to be a payroll with us today, but they sent that on ahead on an earlier train. All I got with me here is some postal monies."

"Then give me that!" Hawke ordered, his square face dark in anger.

"But that's a federal offense, sir!" The clerk was ashen now. "And it's not enough to be worth tangling with the U. S. Government over."

Hawke glanced out the open door of the baggage car in time to see Ringo lose his grip as his motorcycle hit a large rock in his path and he and the machine abruptly parted company. Rawlins grinned a slow, maddening grin that made him appear all the more demonic to the terrified clerk. Hawke groaned deep in his throat and set blazing blue eyes back on the clerk, Hawke's lean, muscular body almost electric with the energy that shot through him when he was thwarted in his aims.

"Goddamnit!" Hawke exploded, "give me the money!"

Startled by his new outburst, the clerk scurried to comply, his thin frame bent double as he crouched over the old safe that sat in the corner. Within a few seconds he returned timorously to Hawke, holding a very small brown leather pouch.

"How much is it?" Hawke fumed.

The clerk licked his lips nervously as Hawke took the soft pouch from his hand and it jingled softly during the exchange. "If you'll remember, sir," he began quietly, "I warned you it was not much."

"How much?" Hawke was quickly losing his patience with this man in spite of his philosophy regarding most people who got tied up with working for the railroad in some capacity.

Taking a quick, short breath, the clerk gulped and spit it out fast. "Sixteen dollars and thirty-seven cents."

"What!" Hawke's face turned red, the black hairs of his eyebrows standing out in a startlingly unusual frame for stormy blue eyes. "Let me see that safe!" He elbowed the clerk aside as Rawlins continued to hold his gun on him, and bent to take a good look inside the safe.

Hawke turned on his heels where he squatted before the safe

to glare at the clerk. "Where's the rest of it?" he demanded. "Or are you one of those heroic types planning to die for the company's money?"

"No, sir!" The clerk refuted Hawke's accusation, stepping back before the strange man in black, worried by the heights of his wrath.

The look of sheer terror on the clerk's face was enough to convince Hawke he was telling the truth. There was no more money on this train unless he wanted to work his way up front and rob the passengers. He would almost have considered it, but he did not figure they had the time. Hawke swore loudly and almost threw the offending pouch of money down, but then reconsidered and pocketed it. They had done better the last time when Jackson had allowed half the money to be blown away on the wind.

"That there's a federal offense," the boyish clerk repeated solemnly, regaining a bit of his nerve when Hawke did not actually shoot him.

Hawke ignored him. "Let's go," he said to Rawlins, who seemed to be taking the entire episode philosophically, as usual.

When they reached the door, Hawke spotted Pronto still working his way slowly forward toward the engine. He had only a short way to go and Hawke swore again.

"Jump," Hawke ordered Rawlins. "I'll turn Pronto back."

Hawke climbed up top, assuming Rawlins had done what he told him, not noticing the man casually continuing to lounge in the car's doorway as he moved across the tops of the other cars. Moving rapidly, his body doubled against the wind, Hawke managed to get up alongside Pronto before he reached the passenger car. Waving his arms frantically, Hawke signaled him back, and luckily, Pronto glanced up in time to see the signal. He waved acknowledgment and started to let his machine fall back as the train pulled forward. Before jumping Hawke ran along the roofs, back toward the baggage car where he could be a little closer to the earth.

When he climbed back down and into the baggage car he

found Rawlins waiting for him, and the clerk still appeared considerably more than just nervous. At the sight of Rawlins standing there Hawke muttered under his breath, but said nothing directly to him. Now was not the time for arguing. Without another word, Hawke jumped clear. Rawlins was right next to him as they hit the ground in unison and rolled.

Instantly, Pronto and Hart Jackson pulled up alongside them as Hawke and Rawlins climbed to their feet unhurt. A few seconds later Ringo, having picked himself up and restarted his motorcycle, roared up from the east. Nobody said a word about his brief absence or the dust that caked his white hair and coated his clothes.

"Let's get moving!" Hawke called out.

Rawlins hesitated, looking from the men to the motorcycles they sat, and the obvious absence of one of the machines, Hawke's Indian.

"Climb on behind," Hawke gestured to the idling motorcycles. "You've got to get back to your horse," he reminded Rawlins irritably.

Rawlins finally nodded his hesitant acceptance of the situation. He and Hawke climbed up behind Jackson and Pronto. Neither one was inclined to take a seat behind Ringo.

They rode hard back the way they had come and managed to progress without further mishap to where they spotted Rawlins' horse standing calmly in the distance, eying their approach, ears pricked forward. Some distance away, Rawlins climbed off the motorcycle and went to rejoin the animal while the others split up as they had planned and headed for the surrounding hills.

"We'll meet in Silver City," Hawke called over his shoulder to Rawlins. "If you make it that far in time."

"Silver City," Rawlins agreed and rode for the old camp where he had left the wagon and other horses.

Moving efficiently, and planning as he moved, Rawlins hitched up the team and tied the horses on behind the wagon. There was one more shortcut. The Notch. He would head for the Notch, skirt the mountains behind it, and take the cut through the mountains into Silver City. Only a couple of spots along the way might be kind of iffy for the wagon, but there was no doubt in his mind that he would make it through all right.

Rawlins sat down to drive, and drive he did, his pace steady, the team pulling well together. Night was only a brief rest-and-eating stop, and he was moving again through country he knew like the back of his hand.

It was midmorning the next day and Rawlins was ruminating on why he had not told his companions about the shortcut when he heard the steady drone of the Indians' engines as they came up over a low rise to the north of him. He would have told them had they been running and needed it, but it seemed to him that a man had to have a few secrets just in case. Besides, there was more to covering a trail than just speed. And more to moving swiftly than those newfangled machines could provide. He could see all their heads turn in puzzlement in his direction as one by one they realized it was him. Rawlins chewed on his tobacco and kept the wagon moving.

Hawke could not believe what he saw when his eyes fell again on Rawlins so soon. How had he gotten through the mountains with the wagon so swiftly? The fact remained that they would reach Silver City well before Rawlins at the rate he was moving, but how had he gotten ahead of them in the first place? There had to be another shortcut Rawlins had neglected to mention to them. Hawke decided he was going to have to have a serious talk with Rawlins when they all reached Silver City. Hawke was surprised to find himself believing Rawlins would actually be there to meet them. Rawlins was a good man to have on his side, as Hawke had always known, and possibly he was the most valuable in his bunch. And just lately he was discovering resources in the man he had never known existed.

CHAPTER 8

What Hawke was trying to prove, not even he was sure of as the machines, somewhat dusty and banged up now, labored under the burning pace he set. Though no pursuit of any kind had developed since taking their leave of the train, the riders clung together in a tight-knit group with neither a protest nor a comment to make on the situation. It was doubtful that word was even out about the robbery, such as it had been. And seeing Rawlins plodding along ahead of them less than an hour before had done nothing to lighten Hawke's mood after the robbery fiasco in which the haul had been sixteen dollars and thirty-seven cents. All Hawke wanted to do now was to put as many miles as he could between themselves and the scene of their ignominious victory over the railroad. And that was exactly what it had been, a victory, no matter how small, but without honor. The blow they had struck would hardly be more noticeable than a flea bite. The operation had not gone efficiently nor according to plan. Hawke wanted some time to sit over a cool beer and give the situation additional deep consideration. He consoled himself with the fact that it had been the first run with the new machines, and nothing could be perfect the first time.

That was part of the problem, Hawke decided, as they jounced and jostled over the rough land until their teeth nearly rattled in their heads. Something inside was trying to warn him that it was only a very small part when they were suddenly possessed of another problem. An abnormally loud pop sounded to Hawke's right and when he glanced in Jackson's direction, he saw the rear tire suddenly droop and flatten beneath the combined weight of the machine and Jackson. The motorcycle slowed and abruptly stopped.

Hawke swore with great enthusiasm under his breath as he circled his machine back to Jackson with Ringo and Pronto trailing. It was an annoyance, but not too much of a surprise. The man Hawke had bought the cycles from had warned him that it might, on occasion, happen in rough, rocky country such as this, and Hawke had a repair kit strapped to the back of each machine. Now was as good a time as any to apply the knowledge the man had imparted to him. What Hawke still had no way of knowing was the fact that it had been an out-and-out miracle that not one of the tires had gone out on them until now, and it would be nearly as large a miracle if another did not blow within the next mile they covered. With the newly developed machines blowouts were a fact of life, but not one anyone really liked to admit to. The manufacturers just sold the materials to repair the holes with for that possible emergency.

Muttering under his breath, his foul temper not in any way helped by the aggravation, Hawke braced the wounded machine up between a couple of large rocks and hunkered down to get to work, the other three men staring in rapt attention as he proceeded.

Sitting back on his heels, Hawke paused in what he was doing. It was going to take longer than he had anticipated. "Why doesn't somebody go shoot a rabbit or something?" he asked. "Might as well have some grub and make ourselves comfortable. We're gonna be here a while."

Pronto rose to the challenge, bouncing to his motorcycle and buzzing off into the surrounding hills, the sound of his engine echoing across the open country. Hawke resumed work, with Ringo and Hart Jackson still looking on. A few minutes later the sound of distant shots drifted to their ears, then the far-off grumble of the motorcycle's motor rolled in from between the low hills to the north. Hawke was still bent intently over his work when the sounds of the engine grew to a roar and Pronto came to a dust-rising, tire-rubbing halt only a few feet away, holding his rabbits aloft for everyone to admire as he dismounted. No one did.

Disgusted with the lack of thanks he got for bringing back two nice plump rabbits, Pronto moved to start a fire, clean the rabbits, and spit them. A short time later the smell of the cooking meat drifted sweetly up in curls of smoke. While dividing his time between tending the cooking meat and observing Hawke's slow progress in fixing the ailing tire, Pronto was the first to spot the small speck in the distance, growing larger with each passing minute.

Screwing up his eyes to see better, Pronto peered impatiently into the distance of their back trail trying to make out who it was. Then, suddenly, it was clear. Swearing excitedly in French, Pronto jumped up, waving his arms in the air as he recognized a wagon leading a cluster of horses tied on behind. Only one man could be coming steadily down their trail like that: George Rawlins.

The wagon and lone rider came on at the same unwavering, steady pace, the wagon rumbling softly over the ground as it was drawn to a halt alongside the disabled machine.

Chewing slowly on his tobacco, Rawlins could not suppress a grin. With reins dangling loosely in his hands and aware of the horses tied on behind, fidgety at the mere sight of the motorcycles, Rawlins spat to one side, then spoke.

"Hoss got a sore foot?" he asked quietly with a wry grin lifting his face.

Salvador Hawke was not without his own well-honed sense of humor, but at the moment it was in mothballs. He looked hard at Rawlins, patient at least initially, with the other's odd humor.

For his part, Rawlins could not resist prodding further. He stared at the tire where it had been returned to the wheel, but not yet pumped full of air. "Couldn't ya' just turn it over and use the round side?" he asked innocently.

It was hard for Hawke to tell whether Rawlins really meant it, or if it was more of his dry humor. But either way Hawke did not care much for the comment, and he let Rawlins know it with a look.

Rawlins continued to regard him with an implacable grin spread across his face, brown eyes glittering. "Want the spare soldier in back?" He indicated the fifth Indian motorcycle he was hauling around the countryside without having put so much as one mile on it in the intended manner. "Be glad to make a loan of it to ya'."

Irritably, Hawke bent back to his work. "I'm almost done here." He tried to sound offhand. "Won't need that loan you offered."

Rawlins sniffed the cooking rabbit and glanced up at the sky where the sun had traveled not much past the nooning hour. "You boys are makin' camp kinda early, ain't you? Reckon with them fine machines you figure you can take it kinda easy."

A little raw from Rawlins' ribbing, Pronto fell into Rawlins' word trap like a green kid, which was how he got himself into most of the scrapes he had to get pulled out of.

"This wasn't nothin'," Pronto slid slightly into his French inflection, indicating the crippled motorcycle. "I was going to go out after some fresh meat anyway." He indicated the sizzling meat over the low fire. Then, magnanimously tearing a hunk of meat from one of the spits, he handed it to Rawlins. "You must a' been pushin' it pretty hard to catch up with us," Pronto commented, in spite of the plainly fresh appearance of the horses. "Bet you been livin' on hardtack and jerky."

"Much obliged," Rawlins replied, accepting the juicy meat and skirting Pronto's innuendos. "My pa always told me to eat when a man offered it, the next chance might not be coming any time soon." He paused, glancing at Hawke where he feverishly worked the small pump, huffing and puffing, his deeply lined face turning beet red as he forced the air back into the deflated tire. Mentally, Hawke swore at the diminutive pump that replaced the air in the tire at a rate comparable to chilled molasses leaving a jar, but lacked the additional lungpower to give voice to his complaints, which was just as well.

Rawlins spat out his plug of tobacco and took a big bite of the hot rabbit, juice running down his chin in a warm trickle. "Well, you boys keep on a'doin' what you're doin'," he said encouragingly. "Reckon I can still make a good piece before dark yet. See you in Silver City." Holding the meat in one hand and flipping the reins with the other, Rawlins started off again, his course south by southwest in about as direct a route as he could choose to their final meeting point. "Now don't forget to bring along my share of that last train we took," he called back over his shoulder with a low chuckle rumbling in his chest.

Hawke was not amused by Rawlins' parting shot, but he was making progress with the stubborn pump and contrary tire. Air was creeping into the void with each press of the pump, slowly rounding out the shape of the tire once again. They would finish here, rest, partake of the mouth-watering rabbit Pronto had brought back, and still pass Rawlins with ease only a short way down the trail. It seemed as if the Fates had been conspiring against Hawke of late, but he was undaunted, secure in the positive knowledge that the machines would be proven superior in the end.

Silver City. The very name used to bring to mind in a rush, a town vibrantly alive, people everywhere, and wild talk about silver strikes nearby and gold farther up in the hills. And that was exactly what it had been for the most part, talk. Silver City had had its day, but this was not it. The town was much quieter even than Salvador Hawke remembered as he and his boys idled onto the main street, horses on either side rolling their eyes and doing a panicky sidestep in spite of their efforts to keep the noise to a minimum.

Curious onlookers gathered on both sides of the street as the Indians and their riders purred with a mechanical growl in the direction of the saloon. Adults watched with an intentness approaching open staring, and children gawked unabashedly. Horses, on the whole, seemed to be of one united opinion. They wanted no part whatever of the strange rolling contraptions that made all the noise. As long as Hawke and his men were in town, it was evident they would have to leave the motorcycles parked somewhere and hoof it themselves. If they continued to create such havoc by their mere passing as they created now, they would not be very popular in town. A few of the horses jerked free of their loose tether at the hitching post and trotted with heads held high, ears pricked and eyes wild, for the edge of town. Owners, spotting their mounts leaving without them, took off in

hot pursuit. A few of the smaller children started to cry and set
off a wail that, combined with the continued snorting and whinnying of the frightened beasts, could have shattered glass.
Women turned away in disgust at the heavy cloud of dust that
was raised by the passing machines along with the distinct smell
of gas fumes hanging in the dust-scoured air. A couple of older
boys started chasing the motorcycles down the street, yelling at
the tops of their lungs and cavorting behind them while mothers
angrily ordered the boys back off the street.

Hawke turned a deaf ear and a blind eye, making himself ob-
livious to the erupting surroundings as he continued slowly for
their destination. Another point was the simple fact that they
would continue to draw too much attention if they continuously
started up the machines for one small reason or another. Hawke
knew there was a small amount of gasoline available in town;
that was partly why he had chosen it as his destination. It was
his intent to get some fuel and wait for George Rawlins to put
in his appearance—that was, if he was not there ahead of them,
a feat that Hawke believed was entirely possible.

As it turned out, it had taken them longer to reach Silver City
than Hawke had anticipated. The trail through the mountains,
desert, and rivers had presented a few obstacles to be sur-
mounted. The trip in all had taken better than six days. Remembering the way Rawlins had performed in the past, Hawke had
had a horrible feeling that he would be in Silver City waiting
when they arrived, and Hawke had not been looking forward to
the possibility with joy. After the first flat tire thay had not seen
Rawlins on the trail again. It had been as if he had vanished off
the face of the territory. At first Jackson had picked up plenty of
wagon tracks, and then, somehow, they had managed to get in
front of Rawlins and the tracks were no more. At least Hawke
hoped they were ahead of him, and Jackson swore that was the
case. Still, until they had actually reached town, Hawke had
not been sure. In town he could see no sign of Rawlins or the
wagon he had been hauling along with the horses tied on behind.
It was a relief Hawke had not been sure he would be permitted
to feel as they had fought their way across the trail between here
and Auton Chico.

After the first flat, things had gone pretty smoothly on the trail, except for the unsettling fact that Rawlins' tracks had disappeared. Once they had hit the trail again they should have passed him easily, but he had mysteriously dropped from sight, though Jackson claimed to have spotted him once in the distance taking a slightly different route. With the wagon to contend with, Rawlins could not use the same one used by the motorcycles. The thought had cheered Hawke, hoping the alternate route would slow Rawlins even more and bring them into town days before him, as Hawke had planned all along. That, if nothing else, should help prove to Rawlins the superiority of the machines to his beloved horses.

It had been about then that things had started to happen. Another flat occurred, his own machine this time, and while he had fixed it with a little more speed than the first, having learned from experience, it had been too late to travel farther that night. They had pitched camp and determined to start out fresh the next dawn. Privately, Hawke hoped Rawlins would not be catching up with them again before they pulled out. These mishaps were showing the motorcycles up in a bad light.

The next day they had made good time until they had hit the Gallinas Mountains. Hawke still could not quite believe what had happened there. For almost twenty years they had traveled this country and they knew it as well as the Indians who had walked the land before them, but somehow they had gotten lost. The machines seemed to put a different perspective on things, but the biggest problem had been the trail they had found. It was loaded with sharp rocks and rugged places where their horses had always gingerly stepped across, but where the machines, always keeping both tires to the ground, could not pass. They had taken an alternate route, one they had never traveled before, though Jackson knew of it, and they had gotten lost. Well, not lost exactly, they had known where they were, the only question being how to get where they weren't. They had ended up following a good trail down into a box-canyon maze that had taken several hours to untangle and find their way out of the twisting coils of the mountains' trails. It had been a frustrating experience, creeping along, feet touching the ground most of the time for balance on either side of the machine, following blind trails, scouting and retracing their steps dozens of times before coming out on the far side of the mountains, as they had tried to in the beginning.

Again things had seemed to improve and then, they had reached the Rio Grande. There had been no choice but to cross, and luckily, in Hawke's first estimation, it had not been at flood, The Rio Grande had seemed pretty tame that day, fairly shallow and broad, laying across its river bottom in a sheet of swiftly flowing water. Hawke had led off, crossing the river with a downstream drift that took him at a gentle angle with the flowing water instead of trying to fight his way straight across it. In a slow, steady pace, they had sent the motorcycles into the water one at a time, the water swirling about the wheels as they turned, carrying them smoothly across. They had been a little better than three quarters of the way across when Ringo discovered the sinkhole.

Ringo discovered the sinkhole in the river's soft bed in the most direct manner. He fell into it. The machine had dropped abruptly out from under him, but his manic grip on the handlebars had taken him under with it. For a few frantic seconds bubbles rose in a flurry from the spot, and with a pitiful splutter, the Indian drowned. Ringo surfaced like a belly-up fish, swept swiftly along in the river's grip for quite a stretch until he managed to half flounder, half crawl, and half swim to shore.

The rescue of the machine had not taken long. Hawke had waded out to the spot where the disaster had occurred, looped a rope around the handlebars, and he along with the others had hauled it out to dry land. What had taken the time had been the work of getting the drowned machine to run again, something they would not have been able to do at all with a horse. But, then again, a horse did not very often drown in water that would have come only slightly over its knees. It had cost them a day and a half cleaning the silt from the parts, drying them, and getting the whole thing back together, lubricated with the thick oil Hawke had in his repair kit. It was a miracle the thing ran at all, and Hawke never would be sure how they had managed it, though

Ringo, Pronto, and Hart had seen nothing but unflagging confidence displayed from him.

Then there had been the detectives. At first Hawke could not believe it when Hart Jackscn told him he had spotted the three distinctive riders when he had been scouting. Hawke had not liked it one bit, and what was more, he was getting damn sick of it. How the hell could they manage to show up everywhere they did in the middle of nowhere? They were coming up behind on fast horses was Jackson's report, meaning only one answer to Hawke's question: They had to have picked up their trail at Auton Chico, where they had robbed the train just outside the little town. Using all the craft and guile at his command, Hawke had led the way into the Miembres Mountains with a substantial lead on the pursuing detectives. There they shut off the engines, giving the detectives nothing to guide their progress, and Hart Jackson had done one of his finest jobs of trail-covering while Hawke, Pronto and Ringo had pressed on ahead, pushing their machines and hauling Jackson's with them while Jackson brought up the rear in no great haste, knowing their margin was good. Catching on to the ways of the machines, Jackson made the trail appear as if they had spotted their pursuers and abruptly changed course, heading straight into Mexico. The ruse had worked, and they had lost them as far as Hawke and Jackson, combining their abilities, could tell. Still, just knowing they were haunting their back trail made Hawke nervous. Never had anyone trailing them been so dogged about it. Never had they kept cropping up with such unfailing regularity.

Silver City was like a refuge, like a sparkling spring to a man dying of thirst. A familiar old friend where he could relax and contemplate. Riding the cycles around behind the saloon, they stashed them well out of sight of curious passersby, sliding them in among some old boxes and kegs, using some old sacking to drape over them.

Pleased with the effect, Hawke made for the saloon, unconsciously rubbing a sore spot in his lower back as he walked. Slightly bent over, he slipped through the batwings, causing not a ripple of disturbance. Hawke spotted his usual table empty and sat down, his back wedged comfortably in the corner, the black of his clothes in the dark room shadowing him into a limbo of nonexistence. He liked it that way, there, and not there. The others settled in around the table, and the bartender, without being called, brought them beer all around and a bottle of whiskey along with five glasses. The fifth glass was for Rawlins, and Hawke had little doubt the man would be showing up soon.

In near silence, Hawke and his men drank during the rest of the morning and part of the afternoon and intermittently feasting on beef sandwiches the bartender had brought them. Then Hawke heard an old familiar rumble out in the street. By that time he was pleasantly tight and a bit depressed.

Things just were not going well for them in recent days. There had to be a way to improve matters, but as yet Hawke had not come up with the solution to their problems. Every time he thought he had, more problems than he had answers for kept coming at him. A leader's lot in life, he decided as he downed another half mug of beer in one gulp, was not an easy one. He was pondering the advisability of allowing himself a thorough drunk, acknowledging in his own mind his extreme vulnerability at such a time, when Rawlins stepped in through the batwings and joined them with the gentle infiltrating of his presence upon them like a tumbleweed driven on the wind. His smile of greeting was creased with trail dust.

"Wagon's out back," Rawlins announced as he sat down, accepting the beer the bartender set before him. "And all the horses are in real good shape," he added, as if conveying news of some old and fondly remembered friends. "Been finding good graze and water along the trail. Yep, they're in real fine shape. Just like they had a holiday."

Hawke grunted, the others nodded. Beer foam was clinging to the bristly, bottom edge of Hawke's mustache and he looked like a surly sea lion, something the surf had thrown up.

"Got any ideas on where you boys are fixin' to hightail it next?" Rawlins asked of Hawke.

Hawke shook his head slowly, and while neither Rawlins nor

the others could make out much of his shadowy form in the dark corner, his face completely lost in the darkness beneath his jerked-down hat brim, they were aware of the kind of a mood he was in. Grim, and perhaps a bit contemplative. There had been other times like this, sitting in a darkened saloon, drinking beer steadily, when Hawke had done some of his best thinking. This time, though, not much was happening. His mind was too cluttered with the disagreeable events of recent days to leave room for much more. Still, he knew he had only to relax, to give it some time.

There had been no answer for Rawlins' question clear in Hawke's mind when the saloon doors swung gently open and closed again, admitting a giant of a man into the room. Upon entering, his broad shoulders had nearly filled the doorway, and now they were blocking most of the dim, dust-filtered light that struggled to slide past him in golden stripes on the wooden floor. His hair, combed straight back from his face, was brown and fell about his shoulders like a lion's mane. Authority showed in his walk, and legs like twin tree trunks strained at the seams of his jeans. His eyes were sunk deep in his head beneath heavy brows and he swept the room with an appraising gaze as he stepped fully inside, then turned directly for the table Hawke and his bunch occupied.

Hawke watched his approach without a great deal of interest, figuring he would take the table near them, but Hawke could not ignore the odd tingling that ran up the back of his neck. It got stronger when the man did not alter course, but came on, right to their table, standing there for a moment like a firmly rooted oak before opening his mouth to speak.

"Mind if I join you boys?" the stranger asked, his voice low, commanding in tone. Not waiting for an answer, he drew up a chair and started to seat himself, straddling the chair backward, the chair front across his chest. His gun was prominent on his hip.

"As a matter of fact . . ." Hawke began, but the stranger cut him off, his steady green-eyed gaze seeming to probe the dim light to lock onto Hawke's narrowed blue eyes staring back out at him.

"Name's Cook, Liam Cook," were the words that cut Hawke off. "U. S. Marshal Liam Cook." He opened the side of his jacket, letting the star glint dully in the dim half light.

CHAPTER 9

Ringo sobered instantly. Pronto half rose out of his chair, his hand dangerously near the gun at his hip. Jackson, his mouth set in a grim line, slid his hand inside his shirt to his knife sheath and rested there as Rawlins shifted his position to better it. With his usual aplomb, Hawke took in the entire situation. There plainly had to be more to this than met the eye. No man, especially a U. S. marshal if he was playing with a full deck, would walk into the guns of five men even if the guns were holstered at the exact moment of his entry. He had to want something. Hawke wondered what.

Cook's chilling green eyes swept the hostile gazes that centered on him from around the table and did not look in the least disturbed by what he saw or the electricity that had instantly charged the air at his revelation of his identity.

"Now," Cook went on as if he were at a Sunday social, "before you boys get too nervous, let me point out to you that I haven't tried to take you in yet, so that can't be the reason for my being here. If it was, I could have had plenty of help from three gentlemen I met out on the street this morning. Fisher, Barnett, and West were their names, I believe."

For the first time Hawke felt a bit nervous. "Here?" His voice was steady, not betraying the anger or apprehension the three names brought to the fore. "How do we know they ain't gonna be coming in that door behind you?"

Cook smiled, a lazy, catlike look that softened his face for the first time. "Well," he began evenly, "since I wanted something from you, I, ah, distracted them for a time. But never fear, they'll be back. They were looking for some strange mechanical contraptions, and didn't find them here right off, so I told them to try an old shack up near one of the deserted mines. It's a long ride up there."

Hawke eyed him cautiously, his hand near his gun. "You said you wanted something?"

Nodding, Cook laid his arms across the back of his chair in a posture that would have made grabbing for his gun almost impossible. "On behalf of the railroad and the law, I'm authorized to offer you and your bunch a deal."

"Deal?" Hawke was curious. What was the man leading up to?

"Railroad top man has a problem," Cook said shortly. "And that makes it the law's problem, and it has to do with Mexico, which makes it a *big* problem."

Holding up a restraining hand, Hawke stopped Cook from elaborating on the specific problem for the moment. "Let's just hold up on what this problem is until after you tell us what we'd get out of this if we decide to help you with your problem. Make it worth our while to hear you out."

Cook nodded again. "I can see why you boys would want it that way. Well, here's the deal. I can offer you complete amnesty from every charge the railroads have brought against you—that is, if you give your words not to rob any more of them. And I can get that federal charge dropped against you if you return the money. . . ."

"Federal charge?" Hawke interrupted. "What federal charge? We never robbed the government."

Cook smiled grimly. "The postal service is part of the U. S. Government. But I was on your trail even before that. Got pulled off it by this problem we have. Found you again because of that robbery."

"Sixteen dollars and thirty-seven cents?" Hawke could not believe it, but he had to admit to himself that the clerk had warned them.

"The amount is not important," Cook pointed out. "The fact of the armed robbery is."

"Cheeeerist!" Ringo swore and took another drink.

"Then there is the matter of a small reward to give you a fresh start," Cook ended as if Ringo had not interrupted.

"How much?" Hawke demanded.

Cook shrugged. "Five hundred. A hundred apiece."

Hawke snorted at the amount of money involved, but he was curious to hear the rest. "Go on," he encouraged. "Now would be a good time to tell us what this problem is."

If someone had told Hawke a year before that he would be considering doing something, he did not yet even know what, for amnesty, a clean slate, and a new start with only a hundred dollars thrown in as incentive, he would probably have flattened that person right on the spot. But that had been a year ago, and it had far from escaped Hawke's notice that things had not been going very well of late. If nothing else, amnesty would get everyone off their backs at one time, sort of give them a chance to reorganize.

"Maxwell Keller's daughter, Erin, has been kidnaped," Cook began evenly.

"Law must be slippin' some if it wants our help," Pronto interjected. "Why don't you just go get her?"

"She was taken into Mexico." Cook's green eyes censored Pronto's interruption. "Your job would be to get her back. When she was first taken, I followed the trail part way into Mexico myself, but there would have been a lot of trouble if I had gotten caught, and they had too much of a lead on me. But I did manage to find out, though, that they were headed for a place called Casas Grandes." Letting his gaze sweep the circumference of the table, Cook paused. "Not being with the law, you could go down into Mexico and bring her back."

George Rawlins sat quietly in his seat, listening and remembering. Erin Keller. The name had rung a bell the moment the marshal had spoken it, but it had taken a few minutes for Rawlins to put it together. The name of Maxwell Keller was not unfamiliar to any of them. The man seemed to own half the trains in the western territories. Erin, though; Rawlins knew she should not have been out there all alone. It had been as if he could sense something was going to happen.

"Where'd they take her from?" Rawlins asked, "And who took her? I'd sure like to wring their necks with my bare hands. Anybody who'd mistreat a little lady like that."

Cook looked startled. He focused his chilly gaze exclusively on Rawlins. "You know the little . . . ah, Miss Keller?" He asked the question though he was sure there was no way Rawlins could have met her. Erin Keller had been a sheltered, protected young woman. Her father had not been in the habit of exposing her to the likes of the rough, lanky cowboy who sat across from him.

"We met," Rawlins said with a lazy grin directed at Hawke. "I liked her right off."

It was a hard statement for Liam Cook to swallow. He had yet to meet the young lady himself and was relying on the memory of seeing her once across a room, along with what her father had told him, for a description. But he was not here to argue, he was here to recruit, and if it salved this man's ego and raised him in the others' estimation to have met the "princess of the line," as she was known, then so much the better.

"We don't know exactly where they took her from," Cook answered Rawlins' question. "She took one of her father's carriages out of Santa Fe to go riding, and just disappeared. A search party went out the next day, but they didn't find a thing. A few days after that, they received the ransom note signed by a Ramon Ortega. The man's a bandit on both sides of the border, but he's managed to elude proof until this. But, of course, even after this, if he remains on his side of the border, there would be no way to do anything about it. And the ransom would be enough to let him live in luxury the rest of his days."

"It's that much," Hawke nodded thoughtfully. There were appealing sides to this proposition. He and his men were going to have to do some talking before committing themselves finally, but there were a few details he would like to have ironed out before they reached that stage.

"The five hundred ain't enough for our services," Hawke announced abruptly from the shelter of his dark corner. "We might settle for five thousand."

Cook was unmoved by the statement, his glassy gaze coolly picking out Hawke's narrowed blue eyes in the dim light. "You were paid handsomely all these years you were helping yourself to the railroad payrolls and ore-shipment payments. Your services have already been paid for. The amnesty attests to that."

"Five thousand," Hawke repeated stubbornly, "or my boys and I don't even talk the matter over." It was a monumental bluff. Rawlins, though his expression and posture had not changed, was ready to go pounding out the door in pursuit, amnesty and money or not. And Hawke had to admit to himself that he would not mind being in on the rescue of the railroad bigwig's daughter. It would be an irony he would find hard to pass up, whatever the others decided. Cook though was not aware of the bluff, and that was what would make it work as any bluff worked through the ignorance of the other party.

For a few moments Liam Cook eyed Hawke, the grim lines in his face getting deeper.

"It'll be a lot cheaper than paying a ransom that'll keep a man living in luxury the rest of his days," Hawke prompted.

"All right," Cook conceded at last, "you'll get your five thousand. Maxwell Keller has impowered me to negotiate on his behalf as the law has on its behalf."

"And those detectives," Hawke added, "I want them off our backs, right away."

Spreading his hands helplessly, Cook smiled faintly and shook his head. "Nothing I can do about them. Nothing anyone can do about them until you earn your amnesty. Sorry, boys, but until then you're still fair game."

With a grim twist of his lips, Hawke returned his smile. "All right," he said evenly, "you give us a little time and me and my boys'll talk about it." Hawke dismissed Cook as he would a not-too-adept errand boy.

For an instant anger flickered across Cook's stern face, green eyes flaring, chest expanding broadly with a long, indrawn breath. Then he rose and left the table, sequestering himself at the far end of the bar to await their decision. He was not sure he liked this job. He should be hauling those five into jail somewhere by any means possible, and instead here he was, in a saloon trying to bargain with them. In his estimation an ultimatum would have been better, but his orders had been clear. Any gang with enough sand and savvy to keep their tails clear of the power of the railroads for as many years as they had would have to be able to get down into Mexico and bring Keller's little girl back to the States—that is, if they were of a mind to.

Liam Cook sighed and hunched over his mug of beer. Things were not as easy now as they had been a few years back. It occurred to him that he was beginning to remember the old days with more fondness than he had felt when he had been living through them.

"Well?" Hawke's voice was low and secretive when Marshal Cook removed himself to outside of earshot.

"We have helped young ladies before," Pronto put in, his French soft and persuasive. "This would not be so much different."

"It would mean we'd have to take us an oath that we wouldn't be robbin' no more trains," Ringo objected.

"Robbing trains hasn't exactly been our strong point lately," Hawke reminded them with a grim quirk of the lips that passed for a smile.

"I say we go," Rawlins put in. "In fact, reckon I'll be headin' down that way whether you boys do or not. Robbin' trains I can see, but draggin' that little lady off from home and folks she loves . . ." Rawlins shook his head sadly, "Why, that's criminal."

Jackson, as always, kept silent to the last. "Be about the most honest thousand dollars I ever earned," he commented. "And I ain't never had no reason to steal a person before. Might be real interestin' to try."

Hawke nodded. He had been hoping they would feel this way. It could very well be just what they needed to break the run of bad luck they had been having. Amnesty and a thousand dollars each just within their grasp. A clean slate to start with, and no detectives on their trail every time they turned around. That last time in the mountains had been too close for comfort. Hawke still wanted to give them a good lesson, a chase they would not soon forget, but maybe this was the best way. He doubted that they would stop at following them down into Mexico. Railroad detectives were not bound by the same rules that bound a U.S. marshal. They just kept on coming.

"I know the country down there as far as Barranca," Hawke said. "Casas Grandes is just a little farther south."

"I've been down that way," Rawlins volunteered, "but never that far south. Got to a little town called Espia once, and into the mountains southeast, but that's it, except for headin' into San Joaquin out of Texas quite a few years back."

Pronto and Ringo both shook their heads. "Only know what I've been told," Ringo put in, "and that ain't much."

"I know the country down to Casas Grandes, and all around those parts," Jackson spoke up last, his hard, angular face creased in concentration. Then he grinned, "Bet you didn't know I went down into Mexico every time we split up for a spell. Sure do have some pretty ladies down there."

Hawke doubted that he could be startled by anything Jackson said or did, or said he did. Jackson was an adept thief, slick as fine silk, subtle or forceful. He had been new at it when he had joined up with Salvador Hawke and his bunch, but Jackson had refined his skills while with them, and apart from them. It was as logical to accept he had headed into Mexico as in any other direction. When they had split in the past to elude a posse right after a successful robbery, they had usually parted not knowing which direction each had taken, only sure of the place and date they were supposed to rejoin forces. It had worked well over the years.

"You're going to have to learn to straddle that machine you've been hauling around in the back of your wagon mighty quick," Hawke looked in Rawlins' direction.

Rawlins continued to sip on his beer and look unconcerned. "Don't like machines," he repeated himself.

"Just what do you aim to do?" Hawke had been sure this new opportunity would change Rawlins' mind. Surely he had to see now that he would not be able to keep up on a raid such as they would be planning. Hit and run was the only way to enter Mexico, snatch the girl back, and get back with their skins whole.

"Ain't seen no problem till now," was Rawlins' reply. "I'll be there."

Hawke shook his head. "It's impossible. It was no more than a fluke the way things have turned out until now. There were problems with the machines, bugs that have been ironed out. What you're doing won't work every time."

"The day it doesn't I reckon I'll be on my own," Rawlins countered, not really worried about that day's imminent arrival.

"You sure this ain't all part of some plan that railroad man has to get us killed down there?" Ringo changed the course of the conversation. "Maybe he ain't even got himself a daughter named Erin, and if he does, maybe she's dead already."

The mention of death threw a sobering pall on the brisk exchange at the table. For a few moments silence hung in the air thick as overcooked mush.

"Told you I met the lady," Rawlins broke the silence. "That first day you rode those contraptions of yours, you spooked her horse so bad I didn't think it was going to stop runnin' on its own. I helped her pull him up. And then she told me her name. That means someone else was in them hills 'sides us and them detectives that run ya'll off that day. Probably kidnapped her right there. From what that marshal says, weren't time for her to get nowhere else before it happened." Rawlins paused. "As for her being dead"—his lips compressed into a grim line—"I don't reckon they'd be in too much of a hurry to kill a woman who looked like that, 'specially since they already got her down into Mexico."

For Rawlins, his past statements had amounted to a speech. Usually a man of few words, competing with Jackson for title of most silent among them, his lecture was almost a breakdown of his unruffled reserve.

Hawke held up his hand for silence. "We can debate these questions later, on the trail. That is, if we're going." He glanced from one to the other, already knowing the answer. "Do we do the marshal a favor and get ourselves five thousand in the bargain?"

A general grunt of agreement sounded from around the table, and Hawke settled back in his chair once again.

Rubbing the fingertips of his right hand over his thumb in an old habit, Hawke grunted his own satisfaction with their decision. "All right," he added, "we go." He leaned slightly forward in his chair, into what dim light the saloon had to offer. The square face and firm jaw silhouetted darkly as he brought large hands to rest on the table. He gazed steadily in Marshal Cook's direction for a few seconds until the man glanced his way and Hawke nodded their agreed consent to his proposition.

The marshal raised his mug of beer to them in salute, then sauntered back toward the table. "I wouldn't take too much time thinking about lighting out," Marshall Cook said coolly. "Those railroad detectives I sent off to the mines should be getting back by nightfall, maybe sooner if they're in a hurry."

"We'll worry about them," Hawke said offhandedly. "We've handled them just fine a couple of times already. Those machines of ours can take anything on four legs." Hawke's confidence was infectious, but doubts were hard to overcome.

"Thought I saw him come in driving a wagon," Cook nodded in the direction of where Rawlins sat idly cutting off a chew of tobacco from a fresh plug.

"You did," Hawke replied, seeing no way to gracefully deny it. "Just don't worry about it. We'll get your job done."

Rawlins nodded thoughtfully to add his assurances to Hawke's and started to chew energetically.

Cook shrugged. "Ain't going to be my skin out there in that desert. Wish it was, but it ain't."

Hawke eyed the big man, easily discerning he was telling the truth. There had been nothing assumed or put on about his simple statement. He regretted not being able to storm into Mexico after Erin Keller. "Have anything else for us?" Hawke asked, wanting to make sure they had all the details before they hit the border.

"Only this." Liam Cook sat down his empty beer mug and took a folded piece of paper from his breast pocket.

Reaching out a black-sleeved arm, Hawke received the piece of creased, stained paper, unfolding it gingerly as if it held within the mystery of the ages. When his eyes fell on the neatly flowing lines of script that stood out against the starkness of the

white paper, he saw what he had expected when Cook had
handed him the square of folded paper. The ransom note.
Hawke had never seen one up close, but it said what anybody
might expect, making dire threats on the health and life of his
captive and demanding money, a hell of a lot of money.

"There was a ring sent along with that," Cook added. "One
that she always wore on the little finger of her left hand."

Hawke nodded. So that was what the note meant when it
threatened to send her finger if the kidnaper did not hear acqui-
escent noises within a very short time. Noises the father had apparently already made in preparation of paying the ransom
should all else fail.

"There's something else too," Cook announced quietly, pausing to let his words sink in as he stood towering above the table,
his chilling green eyes glittering unnaturally in the dim light. "If
you boys don't pull this off, if you don't bring her back, it'd be
wiser if you just stayed down there in Mexico. If you come up
empty, all bets are off and I'll be coming after you. And, machines or no machines, I'll get you. Just wanted to give you fair
warning."

"We don't aim to leave that little gal down there," Rawlins put
in, mushing his words around the ample plug of tobacco he had
begun to chew, "so you can save your warnings for them who
need 'em."

Cook did not look impressed with Rawlins' statement. "You'll
find me waiting at Coyote Springs on the border"—he paused
meaningfully—"*if* you get back." Having had his say, U. S.
Marshal Liam Cook turned, and without another word strode
through the door, the batwings slapping noisily at his exit as if
they had just been witness to a dramatic reading.

Hawke gazed after the marshal's impressive exit a few moments longer, then rose, signaling his men to use the back door
and stealth for their leave-taking. They did not need the whole
town to witness their departure and the direction they took. Still,
it was not going to be easy, not with the racket those cycles put
up when they kicked them into life and the engines began to
throb in the mountain stillness.

Outside the saloon, Hawke paused, glancing from the well-hidden Indians to the wagon Rawlins drove with their horses tied on behind, fresh-looking as if they had spent the days frolicking in tall grass. Hawke felt a momentary twinge of guilt when he looked full into the face of his once-faithful mount, the animal gazing at him eagerly, head erect, ears pricked forward.

Salvador Hawke was a man with pride, but he was a man with good sense as well. They, and that included Rawlins, all needed a good lead on the railroad detectives if they were going to do any good, and the way to get it was as plain as the wagon parked there. Rawlins chewed and waited. Hawke had the irritating feeling that the man knew what was going through his head. Maybe he just recognized the logic of the situation, but whatever it was, Hawk would have been just as satisfied if he had not.

Hawke bit his tongue against the words he knew he must utter, but it did no good. Good sense prevailed. Mrs. Hawke had not raised her son to be a fool.

"Okay, let's load 'em up and get out of here," Hawke announced. "Jackson, see what you can do about wiping these tracks out back here and meet us about three miles east of town. We'll head south from there."

Not one of Hawke's bunch showed any surprise at his decision. Jackson moved to obey the order without question. What Hawke was attempting to do was obvious. If they could clean up the tracks here, motorcycle as well as heavily laden wagon and get the wagon on the trail where other freight wagons had passed before it, their trail would disappear into thin air. Hawke shuddered to think of it, but without the wagon Rawlins had brought along, it would not have been possible.

The motorcycles loaded, Hawke, Ringo, and Pronto piled into the back on top of the poking, jabbing metal and pulled the tarp over themselves. Rawlins pulled out at a sedate pace, leaving Jackson behind to do the job he did so well.

With each bump of the wagon Hawke swore under his breath as one part or another of one of the motorcycles jabbed him unmercifully, but they could not risk being seen. And Ringo and Pronto were not having any better a ride than he. To all intents and purposes they had to appear as a wagon plugging its way up to the mines carrying a load of supplies. Three miles. Three miles they had to travel. Hawke was measuring the distance foot by foot from where he lay sprawled beneath the tarp. Up front, Rawlins whistled suddenly as they rolled along.

CHAPTER 10

As the wagon rolled slowly along, it rumbled and groaned while the horses drawing it labored under the suddenly increased load. Rawlins alternately whistled and callled out low encouragement to the animals as they jounced along, dropping first one wheel into a hole, then bouncing another over an unyielding rock. From where Hawke lay, tarp lifted just enough to see out, watching Silver City disappear in the distance behind them lost in the clutches of the far mountains, he could have sworn Rawlins was doing it on purpose. With a wayward handlebar poking him in the belly, one knee resting uncomfortably on some wheel spokes and his other foot wedged between two of the heavy machines, he swore effusively. Even though they were clear of town and out of earshot of possible passersby, Hawke kept his voice low, muttering only to himself, damning Rawlins' driving to the heavens and swearing to himself that he would find a way to get even someday. Beside him, Hawke could hear grunts, groans, and occasional sharply muttered oaths, a few in French, a language he never had occasion to master.

It was not easy trying to focus on anything, peering out from beneath the canvas, between the string of horses Rawlins had tied on behind the wagon while being jostled and jabbed so often he felt like he had been in a Saturday-night saloon brawl. But Hawke continued to attempt to try until Rawlins pulled up the horses, bringing the wagon to a halt.

"All clear," Rawlins called over his shoulder to his human cargo. "Reckon this here ought to be about three miles like you told Jackson." He rolled the tobacco around in his jaw, then spat, "Best get them things of yourn unloaded."

After Rawlins impatiently flipped the canvas back, admitting the glaring afternoon sun, Hawke sat up and slid off over the side of the wagon. Barely able to stand up straight, he walked a few stiff steps one way, then back, trying to work the kinks loose before he could even think about climbing on top of one of the motorcycles. Pronto bounced off the back end of the wagon, staggered a couple of feet, and found himself clutching the mane of the nearest horse for support. Ringo just hung over the side of the wagon, a dazed look on his face and trying to shield his eyes against the glare of the sun, moving no farther.

"You boys want to unload them things," Rawlins prodded again. "I best get myself a head start, seeing as how fast ya'll plan to be travelin'."

"You heard him!" Hawke snapped, his voice filled with false bravado. "Let's get these things unloaded before Jackson shows up."

It was possible, Hawke reasoned, that some good old-fashioned hard work would help to loosen them up and take out the kinks caused by the rocky, potholed miles. Hawke muttered to himself as Ringo and Pronto joined him somewhat stiffly. But Rawlins made no move to climb down from his perch atop the driver's seat to give them a hand unloading.

Considering the amount of grumbling and groaning involved, the unloading took a very short time. Only minutes, in fact, though it seemed more like several hours to the bruised workers. Before they finished, Hart Jackson had appeared on the sun-baked horizon, dog-trotting steadily in their direction with his usual unerring homing instinct.

Like so many soldiers at attention, the Indian motorcycles were lined up, apparently none the worse for their ignominious ride in the back of the wagon. They had begun to unload Rawlins' machine as well, but he had stopped them with a simple statement of fact.

"I ain't gonna put that thing back in the wagon by myself. You haul that thing out an' I'll let it rest where it sits."

It had not seemed like the time or place to be having another one of their ludicrous discussions regarding the motorcycles, so Hawke had left him and the canvas-wrapped cycle in the wagonbed alone. They had a job to do, and it had to be done fast. This was the time it would finally happen. This time Rawlins would not show up at the right moment, or even the wrong one. The gas supply was fresh in their tanks and Hawke was sure they would have enough to carry them through. Perhaps, if Rawlins moved quickly enough, he could be over the border in time to let them top off their tanks on the return journey.

Closer now, Jackson came on at an even, unfailing trot, showing no signs of exhaustion or even being mildly winded by his near three-mile run. He moved with a rhythmic, almost savage grace, feet taking bites out of the dusty earth, throwing up puffs in his wake. Sweat lent an even sheen to his exposed dark skin, and muscles stood out in cords along his shoulders and neck as he continued the pumping action with lightly clenched fists that appeared to carry him along. His enforced pace slowed by degrees as he approached the knot of waiting men, letting his body naturally gear back down to a more normal pace. By the time he reached Hawke, Ringo, and Pronto where they stood waiting, he looked no more distressed than if he had taken a brisk stroll around the circumference of the town.

Rawlins nodded to him in brief greeting, then lifted the reins, snapping them lightly over the backs of the horses, starting them out at a brisk pace in a southerly direction. With a sense of loss, the other four men watched the departure of George Rawlins. None believed he would be able to keep up with them this time. He was not familiar with the country, as Jackson was. There would be no shortcuts. There was only one way to reach Casas Grandes, and that was the long way.

At a signal from Hawke, all mounted their motorcycles, bringing the machines to life with a combined roar that sent a covey of quail rising up out of a clump of brush a few yards away. For a few moments, Hawke sat the machine on the crest of the low hill, gazing off to the south toward the mountains that jabbed into the azure blue of the sky from the desert that rolled from the giants' feet. It was a sweeping panorama of stark mountains, sandy hills, and a golden expanse of desert, embroidered with a crazy quilt of vegetation that shimmered and wavered beneath the brilliant afternoon sun.

Once again Salvador Hawke experienced that all-encompassing awe generated by the machine he sat astride and the wild country that opened up before him in virgin land. Land never before touched by the wheels of man's progress. He felt and relished the throb of the machine between his legs, pulsating like a thing alive, vibrating with a bottled-up energy that Hawke could release with no more than a movement of hand or foot. The self-doubts and half fears regarding the success of their mission melted away as the winter snow before the coming of the spring sun. If he had been a poetic man, he would have sworn the air smelled a little sweeter, filled his lungs a little fuller, and the sun shone a little warmer against his flesh as he throttled forward and released the brake, lifting his feet off the ground in the same movement. Dust and sand erupted in a fountainous spurt from beneath the rear wheel as Hawke released the straining Indian with a pop and a lunge that sent him downhill in a headlong dive. The start was not quite as dignified as he had planned, but it lacked nothing in power, excitement, and plunging determination.

Hawke stuck with the motorcycle's erratic descent, and behind him he could hear the combined roar of the other machines as they followed suit down the easy slope of the rounded hill. Once again they swung past Rawlins in a body, machines roaring full tilt, nubby tires tearing up the earth as they swept past. The days of the metal rim and the wooden wheels would soon be gone, Hawke had no doubt of it. And he was going to be among the first to help usher it out. With the wind rippling through his black hair beneath the brim of his hat, threatening to lift the hat by the brim, and his square jaw set, Hawke set a southerly course for Mexico and Casa Grandes.

Throughout the rest of the day they rode in a loose knot, almost in formation, like a troop of cavalry. Jackson scouted ahead with a finesse and manner that made him appear as if he had been born atop the machine he rode. Watching Jackson maneuver on the Indian was becoming almost as interesting as seeing a stage show or maybe, years back, visiting the Birdcage Theater in Tombstone. He took curves with a gentle swing, one leg extended for balance and support. Hills, rock-strewn or bald, he usually took standing up, the machine bucking beneath him like a green bronc. Jumps such as they had taken that day, early after they had gotten the machines, he took with ease and no hesitation. Of course, he had gone down a time or two, as evidenced by the small rips and plastered dust of his clothes, but he had said nothing about the small mishaps and neither had anyone else.

Hart Jackson was developing into the best rider among them. The only one with a better record of staying on the back of his machine was Hawke himself, but then Hawke had to admit that he did not pull some of the slick maneuvers he had seen Jackson going through in the distance more than once.

It was not until it was too dark to spot the rocks on the trail ahead that they stopped and made camp for the night. Hawke muttered to himself over the absence of a moon. He had seen many a night when the light of the moon alone had cast enough light to travel by. And now, with these machines, many more miles could have been traveled during the moonlit hours.

As things stood, Jackson did one more sweep of the perimeter of their camp as Ringo got a fire started, then came in, shutting down the engine of his machine with a loud mechanical sigh wheezing through the stillness that settled in around them with the Indian's final cough.

Figuring they would not get many opportunities to hunt, Hawke had made sure they all packed along plenty of hardtack, beef, and beans. In fact, aside from their bedrolls, extra shells, and canteens, that was about all they packed. There was not much room on the back of a motorcycle to be packing along extras. There was, each man had discovered, even less than on the back of a horse.

"Sure could use my saddle long about now," Ringo complained as he leaned back against the meager expanse of the bedroll. He rubbed his arms briskly. "Saddle blanket wouldn't be bad neither."

Hawke ignored the comments. It was just another way to end an uneventful passage of miles, the close of the day. They were all tired, but someone was going to have to stand watch. And this was one time when Hawke would not mind doing it. They had passed the afternoon with no trouble with the machines and no sign of the detectives Liam Cook had spoken of back in Silver City. Hawke was confident, but he did not entirely discount the trio Tom Fisher, Will Barnett, and Sam West. With the lead they had on the motorcycles it should be impossible for the three detectives to close the gap and catch up, but there had been other times during the past weeks when the same thing had seemed impossible and they had surfaced suddenly without warning. Hawke recognized the fact that they would have to be doubly alert from now on. Leaving their home ground, they would be heading into a foreign country and land they did not know. All of them save Jackson. Though he had been with them quite a bit of the time, the man, it seemed, had also been almost everywhere else. Hawke had always known there was more to Hart Jackson than what appeared on the surface. It was probably the Indian in him that made him that way. Quiet in mouth as well as in moccasined feet.

"How far are we from the border?" Pronto asked as Hawke put the coffee pot on the fire to boil.

Hawke shrugged, "I'm not exactly sure, you better ask Jackson. He rode these trails more than a time or two before."

Jackson scratched his chin. "Travelin' like we did today, an' hour maybe."

"When will we be crossin' the Rio Grande?" Pronto asked eagerly.

Jackson frowned, his dark countenance deeply lined, almost appearing like Satan before the flickering fire. "Rio Grande's a good piece east of here. Only cross it if you're headin' into Mexico out of Texas."

"Well, what river *will* we be crossin'?" Pronto pressed, attempting to regain a little of his dignity after his blunder, hoping there was a river out there they would be crossing so he would not have been entirely wrong.

"The Casas Grandes," Jackson said, "and we'll be crossin' when we find a good place. Probably down near Barranca."

"I've been doin' a lot of thinkin' since we left Silver City," Ringo began and Hawke wished the man would not bother to think. It often led to complications where none had been before. "Wasn't there some trouble down near where we're goin' about a year ago? Between the Indians and the Mexicans, I mean. Seems like I heard some talk about a real set-to, a half-ass revolution under a couple of governors who planned on killin' all the Injuns thereabouts. Hear tell there's still a Yaqui-Yori chief down in those parts, a headhunter I heard, goes by the name of Kelzel."

Hawke looked at Ringo in surprise. There was no telling where he had picked up his unique information, but Hawke had heard rumors of much the same himself. A goodly sized band of Apache had escaped into the Sierra Madres in Mexico, Indians who according to the official U. S. Government report did not exist. The Apache had been down there quite a while, apparently not causing any trouble of their own to speak of, when the real trouble broke out.

Pronto made a strangling noise. "Head hunter?" Some of his calm self-assurance had wilted. "Thought all that there trouble with Indians was settled years ago." His flat, angular face was animated.

Filling his plate with beans, Hawke paused. "I don't know all the details of what went on down there, I doubt anyone does, even the ones involved, but the way I got it, it had something to do with some small revolution led by Terrazas and Torres. They recruited themselves a heap of men, some say over fifteen hundred, and bit off more than they could chew. Apache and Yaqui got wind of it and as far as anyone could tell, blew up a powder magazine near a garrison. Anyway, there was a real set-to after that. Indians banded together, even some Americans living down there got themselves mixed up in it. That's how I found out about it. The whole thing was taken care of in about a week, but Terrazas and Torres slipped away. Diaz never did catch up with them."

Jackson nodded in agreement. "We'll be keepin' a sharp eye

out from here on out. Bands of bandits are workin' both sides of
the border now. Some say it's Terrazas' and Torres' men re-
groupin', but whatever it is, cattle rustlin' is big business right
now, that and thievin' of every kind, so folks are just naturally
kind of jumpy."

"What about the Apache?" Ringo pressed. "I heard it was
Cochise's grandson leadin' 'em."

Hart Jackson looked a little impatient, his natural good
humor suffering for it. "It's not the Indians you have to worry
about," he bit out the words. "They're living in the mountains,
farming mostly. Just want to be left alone."

Ringo was not to be swayed. "You speak Apache, Jackson?"
Ringo was not buying what Jackson was selling, at least not all
in one lump. "This whole idea ain't as appealin' as it once was,"
Ringo confessed to the group at large. He accepted the plate of
beans Hawke handed him. Beans Hawke had hoped Ringo
would fill his face with and stop up his mouth, but it did not
work that way. "I never had much truck with Injuns," Ringo
persisted. "Left all that to the soldier boys and them churn-twint-
in', collar-and-tie homesteaders out in hoot-owl hollow." By
now, Ringo was decidedly nervous, and Pronto was getting a bit
edgy.

Having divorced himself from the entire pointless exchange,
Jackson slipped out of camp, melting into the surrounding darkness with the stealth of his own Indian upbringing. Inborn was a
strange, almost sixth sense that warned him of imminent danger,
and it was tingling now. He knew better than to ignore it. In
fact, had they already crossed the border, Jackson would have
sworn there had to be a troop of *soldados* nearby. Automatically, something he had trained himself to do since they had
acquired the machines, Jackson started to translate the miles
their wheels had traced in the sandy earth into hours on horseback. They had left Silver City late. There had been the hold-up
with Rawlins, and the time the others had spent waiting for him
to catch up on the barren hilltop. There had been no trouble
with any of the machines, but Hawke, apparently a little gun-shy
since the last time out, had kept the pace easier, and a bit slower
than before. The surrounding landmarks told the story. The

miles they had covered could easily have been covered by men on horseback, if they pushed hard. It was a fact he did not want to impart to Hawke, but there was no choice. Hawke was not as familiar with this stretch of country as he, and certainly did not yet realize their true position. If Jackson did not tell him what he believed, the surprise could be fatal.

Moving out farther away from the camp, Hart Jackson laid an ear to the ground. Behind him he could hear the low, steady drone of voices from the camp. It was the only thing he had ever had against his riding with Salvador Hawke and the others. None of them ever seemed to have reason to shut their mouths. The monotony of the sound was, at times, almost too much for Jackson to take. Those were the times when his job as scout was the most appealing. Hawke also was a good man on the trail, but it was almost always Jackson who went, leaving Hawke with the others, trying to keep the randy bunch in line. Only Rawlins was as quiet as he, and now Rawlins was no longer with them.

Rawlins? Hart Jackson pondered the possibility, but discarded it almost at the same moment he thought of it. It was not possible for Rawlins to be out there with the wagon and horses. In the first place, what he heard with his ear to the ground meant horses only, no wagon. That ruled Rawlins out immediately, unless he had had trouble and ditched the wagon. The approach, though, was all wrong. It was not Rawlins.

Slipping back into camp, Jackson reappeared out of the darkness wraithlike, the solidity of his body being brought into doubt by the unearthly wavering of it before the rising heat of the campfire. Jackson had not even eaten yet, and his stomach growled a low, protesting note as he snuffed the fire with a deft swipe of his foot.

In an instant Hawke was on his feet, aware that for a moment he had let his guard down, and twentieth century or not, in this country that could be fatal.

"Riders," Jackson announced flatly without being questioned. "Two, more probably three of them. Could be bandits. . . ." he ended with a shrug.

The darkness, though more limiting than on a moonlit night, was not total. A blanket of brilliant stars shimmered overhead and it was in their light that Hawke read the look on Jackson's face, the set lines, the pinched look about his normally sardonically smiling mouth, the far-off glint in the depths of unusually soft brown eyes.

"Or?" Hawke finished for him. "Detectives?" The thought was a ridiculous one when it popped into Hawke's mind, but somehow he suspected there was truth in it, and Jackson had already made up his mind.

Hawke flinched. He was beginning to think in terms of mayhem where the uninvited three men were concerned. Never, in his lengthy career, had he ever come up against anything like them. Their dogged, if not hot pursuit was getting on his nerves. every time he began to feel somewhat secure in their position those three popped up again. Well, Liam Cook had warned them they would still be coming after them until the amnesty was a fact and not a distant goal. Why, it was almost inhuman the way they kept on coming, even in the dark. How could they be trailing them? How could they read the sign? Hawke put the multi-edged question to Jackson.

"Determined men have been known to track with torches by night," Jackson imparted the information with a shrug. "And, as I have told you, it is hard to keep a secret where we have passed. To cover our trail we would have to slow to a pace that would be slower than horseback. Even then . . ." Jackson shrugged his doubts.

"Torches? Then we'll be able to see them from a long ways off."

"If that's how they're doin' it," Jackson acknowledged. "I have not seen, I have only heard. The hills here are close together. The riders are not far off now."

Hawke grinned as an idea came to him. "All right, let's give 'em a nice, warm reception. Get the Indians, and let's get out of here."

"Don't start them," Hawke said sharply as Pronto prepared to do just that. "Push them where I say, and wait for my signal. We'll give 'em a surprise that should give them something to think about on dark nights in the future."

CHAPTER 11

Tom Fisher rode point with Will Barnett and Sam West fanned out behind, completing the triangle. They had been so close in Silver City, so near to drawing the net tight around the three outlaws they had been trailing for such a long time. Close, that was, until that oversized gorilla of a stranger had sent them on a wild goose chase up to the mines. They would have gone all the way up there too if it had not been for one of the miners they had met along the way who had left town that morning just after the arrival of some men riding peculiar machines. Upon cross-examining the man on details, he had claimed the contraptions, to his knowledge, had never left town. Most certainly they had not come that way. And it would have been very hard for him not to notice something like four thundering machines coming up the trail.

There had been no need for discussion. All three had wheeled their mounts and pounded back into town. Through a combination of luck and the power of their railroad connections, Tom Fisher had come up with three fresh mounts while Sam West had been doing the checking and trying to decipher what people told him in conjunction with the few tracks he was able to make out on the roads leading out of town. There had been none of the telltale tire tracks that they had been tracking, and that left only one conclusion. The men had ridden the machines into town, but had had them carried out, and that meant a wagon.

When it came to tracking, Sam West, a man of the land, brown and weathered to resemble the parched hills he had been raised in, was one of the best. When he had swung around the perimeter of the town, eyes the color of a muddy river riveted to the earth in search of some sign while Fisher and Barnett had picked up fresh supplies and extra shells at the store, he had spotted it: the unmistakable double groove of a heavily loaded wagon headed due east. From the way they had been figuring the bunch, the direction was strange, not making much sense, but there seemed little doubt that it was them. Any way a man looked at it, it was a tremendous gamble, but thanks to the stranger with the chilling green eyes that was all they had to try. It was that or forfeit all the work they had done to this point and start all over again.

Salvador Hawke and his bunch had to have known of their presence in Silver City or they would not have left in such a hurry. With that fact self-evident, they would have to move fast if there was any hope at all of catching up with the outlaws. The wagon would have slowed them down for a time, a wagon as heavily loaded as that not being able to move very fast. And there was the additional hope that one of the machines the outlaws now rode would come to a bad end.

Hawke's boys were a slippery bunch, there was no denying that. They had been elusive, almost phantomlike since the very beginning. They had made a lot of friends along the way, though it was difficult for West to grasp how such men could have loyal friends. And very few people who knew the train robbers were willing to give information about them. That, combined with the uncanny ability one of their members had of covering and altering trails, had made West's end of their job all the more difficult. In fact, though his ego swelled at the thought, he was sure Fisher and Barnett, alone, would have lost the trail long before.

Sam West had not been positive he had the beginnings of their trail; it was a gamble they were forced to take. And there had been that feeling in his gut that he was right. The tracks made by the heavily loaded wagon had not been easy to follow, but it was impossible to cover such ruts completely, and once the wagon had reached the well-traveled road to the mines that flanked the other side of the town, all attempts at it had been abandoned. West had been able to follow the logic. Had he not had some idea of what he was looking for, and had they not arrived back in Silver City so soon after the outlaws had pulled out, he probably would not have been able to put it together. As it was, he had followed the road along for quite a way and found the place where the wagon had left the road. The job of concealment of the tracks had been a good one, but West had been looking for the signs and it had opened up like a book to a voracious reader.

Fisher and Barnett had caught up with him then and they had pressed on, following the wagon with mixed feelings. Most of the distance Fisher swore repeatedly at the big stranger who had thrown them off the trail in the first place.

The detectives finally found the place where the machines had been taken from the back of the wagon, and they and it had parted company. Though the wagon and the driver had roused some curiosity, it was Hawke and his boys they were after, and the tire tracks were the spoor of their quarry. At that point West had been sure that they could not have been much more than half an hour behind the outlaws, maybe less. With the animals being fresh and rested, they had been able to push them hard and make good time. There had been no further attempts to cover the four sets of tire tracks, and Tom Fisher had taken over West's chore of riding point.

West had great respect for Fisher's grit and determination. He had never let a quarry slip through his fingers in the past, and he was not about to start now with the most notorious band of thieves and cuthroats they had ever been sent after. Salvador Hawke's bunch had savaged the railroads almost from their inception, stealing and harassing. Others, such as the Wild Bunch, had come and gone, but Hawke was still hanging on. The men in his gang, if they were the original men he had ridden with for many years, all had to be approaching middle age, but that did not seem to slow them down. From the vantage point of his vibrant twenty-four years, Sam West tried to envision a successful bunch of middle-aged train robbers, but could not come up with a mental picture to his liking. The whole picture seemed ludicrous, but Salvador Hawke and his bunch had met with far too much success over the course of far too many years to be even momentarily considered ludicrous in spite of the jumbled relaying of events concerning their last robbery attempts. After all, a string of bad luck could hit any man. Sam West wished he had been on the train the day Fisher and Barnett had had their first close run-in with Hawke and his men. West was the only one of the three who had missed seeing them in action.

Tom Fisher, for his part, had gone into this job with a fanatical determination to bring Salvador Hawke to justice, one way or another. Where lawbreakers were concerned, Fisher was a zealot. Sam West was more interested in the money that could be made in their profession. Being a detective meant more to him than the mere running down of men, as many bounty hunters did. Nonetheless, they had been hired to do just that, and he went about it with the same dedication as Fisher. It was their job. Barnett, for his part, fell in with the plans shaped by the other two detectives.

When darkness had fallen, Fisher had brought out torches, and they had pressed on. Now they were close, very close. While pausing to rest the horses, West had climbed down to examine the narrow tire tracks they had been following. They were fresh, the edges sharp and crisp, not dulled and rounded by the soft night breeze that blew down off the mountains, whipping a darkened chill across the desert lands. Sam West would not have gone along with the idea of tracking anyone or anything in the dark, even with the torches Fisher had thought to pick up in town to aid in the pursuit had it not been for the fact that they were so close. There was that coupled with the fact that those damn machines the outlaws rode could move so fast for a spell. If it had not been for a combination of second-guessing and plain old country-boy luck, they would not have been able to get right on their heels, and now was the time to press their advantage. And press it they would, like a knife sunk in to the hilt. West remounted and they hurried on, this time settling for a brisk walk, hoping the sounds of the night would muffle their hoofbeats.

Salvador Hawke had positioned himself atop a low bluff overlooking the spot where they had been comfortably camped for the night. He straddled his motorcycle, holding it upright between his legs, and listened to a coyote howling mournfully off in the distance. Nearby some doves made soft night sounds where they had roosted for a quiet night's rest. Hawke, irritated by the interruption of his night's rest, did not care one bit for the knife edge of cold air that seemed to slide through him where he sat exposed to the softly moaning wind atop the bluff. At his back was a twin clump of brush, tall enough to mottle his shadow between them and snuff out any sign of his presence that might conceivably be spotted from below. With the night moonless as it was, there was very little danger of his being spotted, but caution always seemed to have a way of paying off. It was the habits a man got himself into that could one day save his neck.

The others were scattered out in a rough circle atop other handy hills overlooking the campsite. They would be waiting, probably more impatiently than he. The plan was simple and direct. The signal to set it in motion was to be the roaring to life of his engine. Ringo, Pronto, and Jackson were scattered, waiting for the signal, probably watching the steady approach of the specks of light as he was. They were carrying torches, all right, as he and Jackson had suspected, and they were coming on strong, the light from the torches dipping, bobbing, and weaving against the blackness of the shadowed earth like fireflies in spring.

Hawke watched them come on, the man shapes growing larger and more distinct astride the dark horses as the distance closed between them. Hawke's vision had always been strong in the dark —like a cat, some men had claimed. And at that point, he would have had little difficulty following the progress of the detectives with or without the torches they were so obligingly carrying to mark their progress. The torches had been a greenhorn move. Those ol' boys could not have been out in wild country too long to be willing to mark themselves like that so they could be seen for miles in any direction. For such stupidity as that alone, they deserved what was about to happen to them.

With a smile that lit up the depths of his blue eyes, Hawke braced himself, then attempted to start the machine he straddled. The engine gave a metallic hiccup, snicked a couple of times, and was quiet. Under his breath Hawke swore sharply, his voice rasping as sandpaper and tried again. The machine heaved, coughed a couple of times, wheezed softly, and gave up again. Though the cool wind still washed down from the mountains over Hawke, large beads of perspiration collected along Hawke's brow as the three horsemen below slowed, then changed direction, heading his way. Hawke swore again, redoubling his efforts. What the hell was the matter with the damn thing? It had never done this to him before. Again Hawke tried, this time twice in rapid succession. The machine bucked, sneezed, and caught, the engine roaring into life with a pulsating throb that shot through Hawke's body to the top of his head.

Almost simultaneously, from the surrounding hilltops, Hawke heard similar explosions of barely controlled power as the Indians barked and roared, the vibrations rippling through the night air, driving the doves from their roosts and silencing the distant coyote that had been calling to his fellows.

Gunning his motorcycle to signal the others, Hawke released the brake and surged forward like a bean out of a slingshot. The hills were alive with sounds of the low, throaty growlings of the machines as they rolled toward the intruders at an appalling rate of speed, the din growing with their approach. It took only seconds for the horses belonging to the detectives to decide what they were going to do. Panic. Co-operatively, the horses followed Hawke's plan precisely, all three of them breaking into terrified whinnies, eyes the size of dinner plates, searching for an avenue of escape. The riders on their backs fought them as the circle of cycles grew tighter, apparently cutting off any hope of fleeing, and the horses began to buck. Jerking heads down between their forelegs against the bit and humping their backs against the saddles, they bucked with all the driving power fear put into their sleek muscles, wanting to be rid of demanding riders, away from the horrendous noise that tore up the night air, and free of the whole damn territory.

With a brief demonstration of their expertise upon the backs of the machines, Pronto and Jackson cut didos around the plunging beasts as the torches were dropped one by one in the rider's determination to cling to his mount, but just as inexorably, the men followed the smoking, smothering torches to the earth.

One of the horses, sleek and brown, hardly more than a shadow in the night, free of rider, reins still knotted around his neck, raised his head and bolted for freedom. Ringo held up his machine a few seconds to let the animal catch sight of the beckoning portal and dash through it head held high, heading for parts unknown. Men swore, animals shrieked, and the machines continued their throbbing roar, seeming all the louder for the tight grouping of them between the hills.

Hawke and his men added to the growing din with yelps and bellows as they continued to run a tight circle around the detectives like a pack of wild Indians, giving none of them time to think of recovering the equilibrium that had been so abruptly stripped from them. The dignity that was hard to regain while sprawled in the dusty darkness on that part of them that rarely saw such abuse.

Gunning his machine with a spurt of gas, Hawke moved to run off the last frightened, puzzled horse dodging past the other cyclists where they continued their tight ring around the fallen detectives. For an instant the animal stood as rooted to the spot as Hawke let out a soul-tearing yell that pierced the rumbling progress of the motorcycles and sent the horse galloping off in the wake of the others. It was then that Hawke spotted Fisher as he reached for his gun, his hand and arm but a shadowy outline. He was pointing the weapon off into the darkness, at whom Hawke could not see. His men were moving so fast astride their machines that he was having a difficult time keeping track of who was where. Engine racing, Hawke changed direction and spurted forward, wheels grinding in the dirt, planning on sweeping past Fisher and tumbling him back into the dust, as Jackson had done with one of the others seconds before. Their adversaries were spread out in a loose triangle, back facing back, a midnight impression of the men who had stood their last stand at the Little Big Horn alongside Custer years earlier.

The rock in his path was something Hawke had not been planning on when he shot his machine forward in a powerful lunge that spewed a hail of pebbles into the air in his wake. The front wheel hit the large rock dead center, lifting the front of the machine. And the back wheel surged forward, seemingly intent in overtaking the front wheel, supplying the momentum for the disaster. In that instant Hawke knew what was happening. He could feel the awful surge as the machine started to rise up to plunge over backward. On impulse Hawke threw his body weight sideways, hoping to at least control his fall as a gun cracked sharply nearby, the report nearly snapping his eardrum.

Pivoting sharply, the machine went with Hawke's weight, careening over on its side with a grinding descent that pinned his leg beneath it and killed the engine at the same time. Killed was not a word Hawke cared for in light of the fact that his leg felt positively mangled beneath the biting weight of the Indian. He preferred to believe it was only resting.

Another shot cracked above the roar of the still-moving cycles and a puff of dust snapped up only inches from Hawke's nose. He could hear his men calling to one another, barking out instructions in the blackness, trying to ascertain exactly what had happened, and to whom, behind the velvet-back cloak of darkness.

Jackson hastily cut another dido off to one side, raising a thick cloud of dust that billowed over the cluster of men and machines, sending Hawke into a coughing, choking fit that threatened to strangle him and coated his eyeballs with a gritty, drying film. Another shot rang out, a motorcycle roared like an enraged beast, someone yelped. The yelp was not familiar and Hawke dismissed the thought that it could have been one of his men.

One of the other machines passed unnervingly close, scattering a spray of dirt, dust, and tiny pebbles in Hawke's face as it roared past. Through the dust and darkness, Hawke made out the form of Pronto riding hell for leather to the core of their little circle, bumping one of the detectives, sending him sprawling again.

With a concerted effort, Hawke gathered himself, jerking the machine beneath him upright and sent life surging through the engine again. Another shot whiffed in Hawke's direction. Then he was moving, his right leg propped up where it belonged, but smarting and burning as he let loose with another wild war cry that rang out above the roar of the Indians. After one more circle of the hapless detectives, flooding them with another thick cloud of dust and rain of pebbles, the outlaws peeled away one at a time, following Hawke, heading for the shelter of the nearest hills to cut off any further possibility of shooting.

Like hornets buzzing a straight path back to the nest, Hawke's Indians roared off into the surrounding hills, leaving the three railroad men to sort things out for themselves. It would take them days to get their horses back or get their hands on new ones, reorganize, and come after them again. Hawke grinned at the thought as a winged night bug splatted against the momentary flash of his white teeth. Hawke spat wildly as they roared around the base of a low hill, pointing their machines once again for the Mexican border. According to Jackson's calculations of a few hours earlier, they should be able to make it by daybreak. By the time those three came after them again, they would be on their way back with the girl and ready for the amnesty Marshal Cook had guaranteed.

CHAPTER 12

Salvador Hawke and his three men pushed on, not with the feeling of power and excitement that had possessed them during the darkest hours of the night just past, but with the droning, unraveling of the miles, the same boredom a man would feel in the saddle of a plodding horse. The sun pounded down upon them, glaring up off the flats that surrounded them now on all sides, the distant mountains seeming no more than a mirage on the horizon. The wind blew incessantly, a hot breath from the bowels of hell, grinding dust and grit into every pore of Hawke's face and each small corner of exposed flesh. He was convinced that if it were not for the steady growing out of his beard, his face would have long since been a frozen mask of grit. They had stopped only briefly for a cold breakfast of hardtack and beef jerky. It was laying there in his stomach now, where he had put it a couple of hours before, like a pointed rock. Pronto complained continuously above the roar of his cycle, of the back pains that plagued him. Hawke did not doubt the truth of what Pronto was claiming, but he was getting damn sick and tired of hearing about it. For himself, every muscle in his body ached after the spill he had taken in the dark. In spite of his tending it when the sun had risen to give some light, his leg had stiffened up. The hide had been taken off the outside of it from just above the boots that started at midcalf, all the way along his thigh to his hip. He had bathed away the dried blood and dirt with precious water from his canteen, and though the peeled-grape look of his flesh was not pretty, it also was not serious, just painful.

Hart Jackson was in the lead now, this side trip being his idea, one that had sounded good until the reality of the flats had made itself uncomfortably clear. The tracks their cycles made disappeared almost immediately in their wake, the wind wiping the earth clean behind their passing. Rippled ridges rose and were wiped away almost at the same instant as the blowing wind shifted direction or gusted unexpectedly, shaping and reshaping the dust that lay in a thin layer over the hard-packed ground beneath. It would seem as if they had disappeared into a cloud of dust and had been plucked from the very surface of the earth. And at this point Hawke almost wished it would happen. He felt as if he were a ripe plum being sucked dry into a prune. He could feel dry creases forming on his face as they roared into the blazing onslaught of wind and sun.

Water holes, according to Jackson's information, were in the distant mountains. It was a thought the rest of them could not help but dwell on.

There also, within the sheltering heights of the mountains, were places, Jackson claimed, where he could leave bits and pieces of a trail that would drive any man attempting to follow them crazy. It would be worth the nearly full day they would be losing to insure against close pursuit. Hawke did not want to look over his shoulder and see a dust cloud again. What they had done to the detectives' horses had been good, but this would make sure. It would keep them occupied if by some twist of fate they managed to get this far. Hawke figured he and his boys could return to New Mexico with the girl by a circuitous route, leaving those three bully boys down here in the desert mountains to chase their tales until doomsday. It was a pleasant thought, and it kept Hawke going. That and the five thousand dollars.

In a ragged line they pressed on, engines droning, wheels skimming over the ground, moving deeper and deeper into Mexico. They rode tense, Hawke, Jackson, and Pronto keeping an eye out for the *soldados,* Ringo with a wary eye directed toward the mountains, visions of Apache on the warpath coloring his thoughts. Maybe it was the twentieth century, and, as Jackson had claimed, the Indians might be farmers now, wanting to be left alone, but Ringo had never had any truck with them before, and he was not planning on starting now. If he saw any spotted ponies on the horizon he intended to head in the opposite direction, amnesty and rescuing the fair damsel be damned. Hart Jackson could palaver with them all he liked. After all, he was half one of them anyhow. His daddy had been a runaway slave, his mama a full-blooded Injun. What tribe had never been made clear, so it might be Apache as well as anything else.

Time dragged as the mountains that had appeared only a few miles away grew slowly and rose out of a brilliant bluish haze directly in their path, still many miles away. They appeared to grow larger as they drew closer, but remained elusive, as if they were no more than a cluster of mirages, moving steadily backward, floating as phantoms before their eyes, drawing them ever onward. Hawke, though, knew better. He was no stranger to the peculiar illusions of desert and mountains. Of the strange relationship between size and distance. The mountains were big, the desert broad, and the distances interminable. The distance it would have taken them days to cover on horseback was now taking them little more than a day, and still the flats, the rippling heat seemed endless. As one, they gazed toward the beckoning coolness the mountains to the east and south of them promised. They were running roughly parallel to the Rio Casas Grandes, and Jackson had made it clear that they would have to ford it. Hawke tried not to think about it. He remembered only too well the last time they crossed a swiftly flowing body of water, the Rio Grande on the way to Silver City.

They stopped briefly in Espia, hardly more than a dimple on the land, and Jackson did most of the talking, asking questions about a young American woman being brought through not too long before. Knowing a few people of the village from his previous visits into Mexico, Hart Jackson had little difficulty in getting answers to his questions, a feat outsiders might have found considerably more difficult.

The cycles caused such a stir in the small village that they were forced to stay for a meal of tortillas, chili, and beans while the combined population—men, women, and children—examined the strange mechanical contraptions that had roared into the quiet of their lives. Watching nervously, Hawke had stuffed his mouth with food while adults and small children alike poked at the rubber tires with long sticks or sidled up close enough to poke fingers where fingers most decidedly should not have been poked.

Still, when they climbed back up on the machines and turned over the engines in rapid succession, the roar of the motors sounding like a cannon barrage, no harm appeared to have been done. And the goodwill of the villagers meant a lot, or it could mean a lot if they came back this way with trouble on their heels. They had gotten the information they sought here and the reassurance that they were on the right path. As far as Hawke was concerned, a U.S. marshal's word was not good enough. He had to know for himself. Cook might have gotten this far, but the villagers would have told him nothing, and he would have been forced to rely on what trail he could find, the direction it pointed, and his own supposition as to what had happened.

The woman Jackson had been talking to had imparted additional information. The young American woman had not appeared to be restrained in any way. But then, where would a woman run in this country, even if she were free? And just because she was not tied when they rode into the village did not mean they had not been putting up a good front for the villagers to enable them to get supplies without question. But why would they care what the people thought? It was a bit of a puzzle, but Hawke was equally sure that though she was not visibly hobbled, there had been someone mighty close by keeping a sharp eye on her actions. It was also noted that she had not moved more than a few paces from the side of her horse when she had dismounted. And a beautiful animal the horse had been. Sleek and delicately boned like its mistress, looking like something that might be drawing a princess's carriage. The description too fit the one the marshal, as well as Rawlins, from his one brief meeting had given of her. The short, plump woman with whom Jackson exchanged a rapid-fire Mexican Spanish had been most impressed by the woman's milky white skin and contrasting blue-black hair. The skin she had been sure would be burned to a crisp beneath the desert sun. The villagers had wondered what such a pretty *gringa* was doing riding with the hardened bunch in such rough, wild country. But it had been none of their affair and they had kept clear of it. A wise move indeed from what Hawke was able to glean from the situation.

Their bellies full to bursting, their thirst slaked, they roared out of Espia in a route that took them almost directly south. The place they were looking for, they had since learned, was not Casas Grandes itself, but a place in the mountains more east than south of it. Some very disreputable sorts were known to headquarter there, and they had received the warning regarding the *soldados* who patrolled on occasion. They had been in the village of Espia only days before, and it was better to avoid them if one was able. Far better.

Hawke and his men camped that night without incident along the west bank of the Rio Casas Grandes in the shadow of the mountains. They pushed on through the next day and just before sunset reached their destination. Jackson had scouted ahead where he could see for long distances. The noise of his motorcycle he kept muffled between slopes, hoping that if it was heard it might be mistaken for the distant rumble of thunder. When he had doubled back with news of his discovery, they had shut down the machines and made camp. The situation from there on was going to be a delicate one. They were not eager to have anyone know of their presence in the mountains until they were ready to take care of the job they had come for and make a run for it. Speed would on their side, but not if the *banditos* could hear them long before they arrived.

First, they would have to make sure Erin Keller was really being held within the adobe walls of the fortress Jackson had spotted. It was hard to envision another such place nearby, but they would have to be sure before they tried to break in. That in itself was something Hawke had not been planning on. It had not occurred to him when he had accepted it that the job would entail storming the walls of a fort obviously built with the original intent of repulsing Indian attacks. Hawke smiled grimly to himself. This was going to be an Indian attack of a a different sort.

It was the first time Hawke had missed Rawlins' presence.

When it came to Injuning up on a place, Rawlins was nearly as good as Jackson, and he had seen the Keller girl once. He would be able to recognize her in a moment, not just guess and hope he was right. Hawke sighed. There was no help for it. Rawlins, in spite of his self-confidence and bravado, was nowhere to be seen. Hawke had known it would finally happen. Stretching out under his blankets, pulling his black hat down over one ear, Hawke shifted in an attempt to find a dent in the earth corresponding to the angles of his body. He would not admit it to anyone, but if the truth be known, he missed his saddle for a pillow every night as much as the next man. The night watch was split. While Jackson was making use of his Indian endowments, Hawke drifted off into an uneasy sleep. All they could do now was wait for daylight.

The coming of dawn brought with it some odd sounds that roused Hawke from a light sleep. He had stood middle watch, and with little sleep on either end, his brain remained fogged for a few vital seconds as the sounds registered themselves, and he took proper note. Propping himself up on one elbow, his gaze swept past Jackson where he was rolled in his blankets breathing deeply in sleep. Then he focused for a few moments on the motorcycles, expecting them to lift their heads horselike, pricking ears in the direction of the sounds and let him take his cue from them regarding the approaching danger, or lack of it. Old habit died hard.

Hawke rolled out of his bedroll, gun in hand, and glanced to where Pronto was standing the last watch. He too had heard the sounds drifting on the crisp morning air. Gun in hand he was poised, waiting. Probably awaiting the same nicker of alarm Hawke expected. Stiff from his night on the hard ground, Hawke waited, listening intently for the faint sounds to repeat themselves.

Then he heard them again. A soft rustling, what sounded like a footfall, and a low, melodic whistling. Ears straining to catch the notes of the tune, Hawke turned a quizzical gaze in Pronto's direction. Pronto looked blank. The notes of the tune were a little clearer now, a little louder. Jackson stirred in his blankets, coming awake all at once, the one among them who needed no time to readjust.

With the strains of "Clementine" drifting before him, George Rawlins stepped casually into the camp, leading a horse saddled and showing signs of exhaustion, behind him. Hawke stared in open disbelief, the disbelief being shared by Ringo, Jackson, and Pronto. The absence of the wagon and the fact that he had with him only one horse were the things that impressed themselves most urgently on their minds. It should have signaled disaster, but Rawlins himself appeared in good health and good spirits. Only the horse he led looked bedraggled.

"Well, I reckon you boys were about half right," Rawlins drawled as he strolled in. "Before I reached Espia it became mighty clear to me that I wasn't gonna catch up with ya'll in time for all the fun. Not with that wagon I was draggin' along behind. So I left it stashed in a valley this side of the Casas Grandes River. Horses have plenty of feed there, and water. They'll be all right there for a spell. Me an' hoss here did all right on our own." He gave the tired beast an affectionate pat. As if searching for a missing object, he glanced around the camp quickly. "You ain't gone and rescued her yet, have you?"

Hawke shook his head, the shock of Rawlins' newest appearance wearing off more quickly than in the past. "We were getting to that," he said with his usual authority. "We haven't even made sure she's in there yet." He made a broad gesture through the trees that separated them from the fortress where they assumed Erin Keller to be in residence.

Rawlins looked a bit puzzled by his statement. "Wherever it is," he said slowly, "she's got to be there. Ain't nowhere else in these here parts for her to be."

Jackson nodded in agreement. Rawlins' logic had always made sense to him.

Hawke's face read like a book. He had to be sure before they tried anything, heroic or otherwise.

"I know what she looks like, seen her up real close," Rawlins ventured. "If I could get a look at her I'd know."

Nodding quickly, Hawke did not bother to admit that he had

been regretting Rawlins' absence for just that reason. "Jackson," Hawke ordered, "you go with him. See if you can spot any weak places. Get an idea how many men there are around. Horses, Guards. Pronto and I will get ourselves up on the ridge overlooking the front gate and do the same. Ringo, you stay here and keep an eye on things. We can't afford any surprises now."

Ringo did not look happy or impressed with his chore, but until all of them decided Hawke could be replaced, his orders were law. Ringo hunkered down on a rock near the center of camp and muttered to himself. In the past he had spent a good deal of time holding the horses, and now it seemed he was going to end up watching the Indians. He was going to have to learn to set that dynamite right, there was no question about it.

CHAPTER 13

There were still a couple of hours of daylight remaining when Hawke and Pronto rejoined forces with the rest of his men back at the camp Ringo had guarded. Hawke had pondered the situation as he and Pronto had lain in concealed observation posts for the long hours that had made up the day. In spite of Pronto's urgings to hit the adobe fortress like a cavalry assault, take the woman, and clear out, Hawke had managed to sort his thoughts. Pronto was direct, if not wise. Between ten to fourteen men were inside those walls. He and Pronto had seen them through the gate that had been opened early in the morning and had still stood open when the two of them had withdrawn. Inside, the men were evidently armed to the teeth and wore grim looks that spoke of the poverty and violence that was as much a part of their daily lives as the bread they put in their mouths.

No, the plan Hawke had come up with was no direct assault. It was more a slight-of-hand. The motorcycles would serve them well. Several times during the hours spent laying on his belly on the hard earth he had seen a woman such as the marshal and Rawlins had described, and he was almost positive it was Erin Keller. He would reserve final judgment though until Rawlins gave his opinion. If they managed to go in after the wrong woman his plan would prove to be a useless exercise in stupidity.

The look on Rawlins' face as he and Jackson approached from the opposite end of the camp washed all doubts from Hawke's mind. They had located the right woman. All there was left to do was to get her out. It would have to be done near dark, they would need the cover of night once things started to roll. Hawke smiled to himself at the analogy, but turned a serious face to his men.

"Jackson," Hawke began mapping out his plan of attack, "you and Pronto take your cycles and set up a distraction. Draw off most of the men"—he gave a tight smile—"all of them, if you can. Watch yourselves, though; these men look like a tough lot."

Jackson agreed with the statement. "Bandits. They're cutthroats who raid both sides of the border. This is their stronghold. A wise man would skirt wide around it."

For Hart Jackson the few words he had spoken amounted to a speech. "There is another entry at the back," he added in the silence that followed. "When we get this commotion going, we'll circle back and come in that way."

Hawke nodded his agreement. "Rawlins, you and Ringo will come with me to get the woman."

Ringo lit up at the prospect. It sure as hell beat holding the horses or guarding the camp.

Shifting his gaze, Hawke directed his next question to Jackson. "I spotted the woman from the ridge, but she didn't appear to be too restricted in her movements. She went in and out of two or three buildings. You have any idea as to which one she might be quartered in come nightfall?"

Jackson frowned deep in thought, his angular face sharpened, his brown eyes turned inward. "Where would she go?" he asked in response to Hawke's remark about her free movements. "Which building?" he shrugged. "I saw her carry what looked like laundry into the second one on the left as you go in the gate. The two-story adobe. The size and lookout advantage would probably make it Ortega's place. Don't see how any of the rest of them *banditos* could be top honcho around here."

Tightly, Hawke nodded. "All right, let's get going."

Pronto and Jackson straddled their cycles, starting them and nursing the cold engines into a vibrating roar before easing them into gear and jerking forward as the tires took a bite into the earth and surged with the power pumping through their gas lines.

In the puff of sand and dust that rolled in their wake, Hawke and Ringo pushed their cycles forward to the ridge without starting them. The sun was heading for the western mountains and a red glow was painting the sky. Sunset was pressing them, but Hawke knew it would be to their advantage. With as many as fourteen guns, probably more, to guard the woman Ramon Ortega had had the blatant brass to snatch from right under her powerful daddy's nose, Hawke knew the urgent need of speed and stealth.

Rawlins led his horse along behind them. He would follow Hawke and Ringo in, provide cover for their backs, and keep an eye on what was happening. Hawke knew Rawlins would never tolerate the thought of being left out of the maneuver, and Hawke was just hoping the man would not manage finally to get himself killed. Once the hornet's nest was kicked over, it was Rawlins who was going to find himself out in the open with nowhere to run. This was not the law they were going to be dealing with. It was a bunch of cold-blooded killers who would not be thinking of taking any of them in for a trial.

What was worse, an angle Hawke did not even want to think about was the fact that if they failed, it could probably mean the woman's life would also be forfeit. A sheep-gutting throat cutter the likes of Ramon Ortega could easily kill her in fury if he decided the crazy men on the strange machines had been sent by her father to prevent payment of the ransom demanded. It was a touchy situation, but there was no turning back. Jackson and Pronto were already moving.

From the top of the ridge above the opened gates of the adobe fort, Hawke, Ringo, and Rawlins could see the show as if they had bought ringside tickets to the circus. Pronto cut a couple of didos in the dust, raising it in billowing clouds around him as Jackson made an aborted run for the open gates. Excitement could be heard from within. Men were shouting and calling harshly to one another as the horses set up a din whinnying and snorting. The animals shifted within the confines of their corral, running from one side to another as a packed cavy on the open range trailing cattle drive.

Under their now experienced riders the machines responded well, giving the occupants of the buildings the distinct impression they were being placed under a siege. By what was the mystery. The two motorcycles howled like a pack of screaming savages and multiplied their numbers by the deception of sound.

Inside the adobe walls men were reacting the way Hawke had counted on. They were running to their excited horses, trying to calm and saddle the beasts. Hawke thought he caught sight of a pale face at one of the upstairs windows of the house Jackson had indicated. It was there, then just as suddenly it was not.

The evening air, usually quiet as the day wound to a close, was electric with excitement, the air building and splitting with sounds foreign to it. With perfect timing Hart Jackson pulled off, allowing the horses inside to calm enough to be saddled. Pronto stuck with him, wheeling off a short distance to the north of the gate and stopping dead as if his machine had been a horse pushed too hard and dropped beneath its saddle. Hawke strained his ears to catch some sign of a double idle, but there was plainly only one: Jackson's. Pronto's motor had died. The Indian was not adding its thready roar to its twin. Jackson had pulled up, circling back toward the disabled Pronto.

Hawke clenched his teeth, narrowed eyes sliding back through the open gates to where the horses were saddled and already being mounted. Pronto was working at starting the stalled machine. Hawke braced himself. The whole thing could go right there. They might get another chance and they might not, but one thing was for sure: The same trick would not work twice.

The first couple of horses were loping toward the gate and through it. The man in the lead, dressed in fawn-colored, skin-tight breeches, white ruffled shirt, and slick knee boots, could only be Ramon Ortega. The man was a rogue, a cutthroat, and a thief, but he sure as hell was a snappy dresser. And the animal beneath him, its hide sleek and glossy, its limbs clean and powerful, stretched out like a Thoroughbred racehorse.

For the moment the men pouring out of the gates wore looks of grim amusement, as if it were all a lark and they were playing a game. No guns were drawn yet, but Hawke had a feeling that that would not last long.

Jackson was stopped in front of Pronto, gesticulating wildly as he spoke. Hawke, poised to start his own engine, swore under his breath as the riders from the fort bore down on the two men. Then, as abruptly as it had snuffed itself out, Pronto surged life back through the engine and nursed it to a full roar, rolling with Jackson as the leaders of the pack that howled like coyotes on the hunt raced toward them.

Hawke watched as the leader's horse did a double take, then rose up straight into the air on hind legs, forelegs reaching for the glowing evening sky at the unexpected explosion of new sound. Ears flattened against his head, the animal proved unmanageable for long seconds as the two motorcycles pulled away, cresting the first hill well ahead of the pursuers.

Glancing at Ringo who, during those tense moments, had produced a thin film of sweat across his forehead, white hair pasted against it, Hawke gave the nod. There was no need for them to start up their engines. It was easy for them to coast down the side of the gently sloping hill, guiding their machines toward the back entrance. Hawke had no way of knowing how many of the bandits had stayed behind, but stealth would obviously lengthen their odds.

Shoving off, they balanced on the machines to the bottom of the slope, letting the momentum of their descent carry them in a broad loop along the rear of the adobe wall. Rawlins waited until they disappeared inside, then followed along behind, eyes and ears attuned to danger. They were going to rescue that little lady, bring her out, but nowhere was it written that it had to be at the cost of their own hides.

The muscles along Hawke's shoulders were bunched as if in anticipation of a blow. Every nerve, every pore, every fiber of his being was stretched taut as a bowstring. He had pulled plenty of crazy stunts in his time, but this was one of the worst. A couple of women, Mexican by their appearance and dress, fled for the shelter of the mud houses at Hawke and Ringo's unexpected, silent, and sudden appearance. The fact that Hawke did not as yet have a gun drawn did not seem to make much difference. Hawke's eyes swept the compound for some sign of men, but came up empty. The adobe buildings were quiet; only a few horses stood in the corral eying their approach. Doors were shut

tight and the single street down the middle of the cluster of mud
houses was quiet. Automatically Hawke counted the horses that
stood tensely in the old corral. Four. He could count on there
being no less than four men left to guard the place until the
others returned. Where, then, were they?

The sky had turned dusky gray with the disappearance of the
sun beyond the western horizon, though a faint glow of daylight
still persisted, filtering across the gray as stray sunbeams shot
upward and the sun reluctantly gave up another day. Hawke and
Ringo pushed the machines the last few yards, parking them in
front of the two-story adobe. Hawke's senses tingled, warning
him of danger close at hand. As Ringo joined him he paused,
glancing through the gathering darkness for some indication as
to what was affecting him so strongly.

Hand resting on his gunbutt, Hawke whirled as Rawlins
bolted through the rear entrance of the walled adobe. At the
same instant Hawke spotted the man standing in the shadows of
the wall and Rawlins bearing down on him. The man shape in
the shadows had been unaware of Rawlins' presence until the
thundering rush of hoops assailed his ears, and then it was already too late. Leaning half out of the saddle, riding like a carni-
val performer, Rawlins cold-cocked the man, dropping him in
the dust where he had stood.

Slipping into the darkened interior of the house, Hawke
turned back to his objective, fumbling his way to the stairs with
Ringo in tow. Ringo had his gun out now, and Hawke was
aware of the gleam of his light gray eyes in the darkness near
him. Rawlins, as before, brought up the rear and he too was carrying his gun at the ready. Hawke remembered only too well the
sight of flame stabbing into darkness as pistols exploded and
hoped he was not about to relive past experiences.

Two at a time, Hawke took the stairs that led to the upper
compartments. He was aware of the coolness of the air buffeting
him softly from every angle, and tensed for the attack that could
come at any turn. Hawke did not believe that even Ortega could
be so sure of himself as not to leave a guard inside the house
with his captive when he was drawn away. At the same time, if

Ortega was keeping her for himself, as a man of his kind likely would, who could he trust to stand watch over her but himself? Hawke shook his head. It was a puzzle that would soon resolve itself . . . one way or another. He only hoped when they reached Miss Erin Keller, daughter of the high-and-mighty railroad man, that she would not be too scared to run. Before taking on the job he had not given much thought to that angle. A howling female could be a real detriment to their making it back across the border in one piece, collectively or individually.

A bit of silvery moonlight cast by a sliver of moon shimmered in through the small windows that lined the hall. Hawke could have sworn that in the distance the sounds of Jackson's and Pronto's motorcycles headed back their way were already reaching his ears, and it could mean more trouble. Hawke increased his pace slightly, moving catlike down the long hall, stepping lightly on the balls of his feet. Ringo was crawling up his back and Rawlins had his head hung over his shoulder trying to see what was coming. It seemed to Hawke that it had to be stuck in that position permanently.

The door ahead of him was closed. Hawke laid a tentative hand on the ornate doorknob, feeling the coolness of the metal beneath his palm as he curled tense fingers around it and slowly began to turn. No sounds came from within, and while he was sure it was the room where he had caught sight of the pale gleam of white flesh from below, he was beginning to wonder if its occupant was still there. Gun at the ready, Ringo at his shoulder, and Rawlins flattened against the wall in anticipation, Hawke twisted the knob and threw the door inward with one fluid motion, crouching low as he launched himself into the room.

Hawke expected an explosive burst of action, a gun firing, a scream, something, but suddenly he found himself crouched near the floor, the fingers of one hand brushing thick carpet that crushed beneath his boots. And he found nothing.

Then there was a shifting, a rustling of fabric, and a low voice reached out across the open space to caress him.

"Are you looking for something?" The voice, melodiously

feminine and touched with a cat's purr, addressed him as if he were not really crouched on the floor near her bed.

Hawke froze where he was. It was not possible that this was the woman they sought. That the calm, soothing voice belonged to a young woman kidnaped from almost beneath her loving father's nose and dragged off to Mexico across burning desert. Dragged by men who had undoubtedly taken advantage of her helplessness and used her in any way that pleased them. The very thought was enough to make a gentleman's blood boil. But the voice . . .

"Erin Keller?" Hawke questioned as the room righted itself in the wake of his awkward entrance and he became aware of a bed, and a form half reclining upon it.

"Yes." The form shifted to sit upright, legs swinging over the side of the bed to put small feet and slim calfs only inches from Hawke's eyes before the woman stood up, white nightgown falling back into place, allowing only small pink toes to peep from beneath the draping hem.

Hawke stood up but refrained from holstering his gun, even though he was concerned that it might frighten her. Had he imagined it or had her voice become a little cooler, a little sharper with that simple one-word reply?

"We came to rescue you, ma'am," Ringo slipped through the door before Hawke could frame a response to the woman's one-word oratory.

Erin Keller stood there a moment, a vision in the darkness, floating before them in a long white bedgown that could have been gossamer. Hair, long and blacker than night, fell heavily about her shoulders in a silken curtain that picked up every stray moonbeam that chanced in through the window. With unhurried calm, she struck a match and touched it to the wick of the oil lamp that stood at the bedside.

"You should have let me ride with you a ways that day like I offered, ma'am," Rawlins threw in from the doorway where he had placed himself like a guard, half in and half out of the room.

Large brown eyes grew larger beneath a sweep of lash and Erin's mouth dropped open at the sound and sight of George

Rawlins, the man she had met so unexpectedly on the trail many days before. An outlaw. A man her father had been pursuing for years. What was he doing here, now? And the rest of them?

"Rescue me?" Erin began. "Rescue me from what?" She knew this should all make sense somehow, especially in the light of what she had done, but her mind was a blank and it did not.

"Ortega," Ringo butted in again. "The man who kidnaped ya and dragged ya all the way down here."

"Kidnaped?" Erin threw back her head and began to laugh. Laughter seemed to make her more beautiful, her milk-white skin flushing with color. "Who said I was kidnaped? My father? I ran away with Ramon. We're to be married. I wrote a letter to father." Erin frowned, the dark brown of her eyes darkening, her full red lips pursed deep in thought. With wings attached, she could have passed for an angel.

"I'm not going anywhere with you," she said firmly. "I know who all of you are. Father has been after you for years for robbing his trains and so have half the other railroad men in the western part of the country. It's you who are the kidnapers. You who want to get something out of my father by carrying me off," she accused, standing firm, arms crossed before her, brown eyes flashing.

"Afraid not," Hawke told her, acutely aware of their shortage of time, half in awe of the situation they found themselves in. Apparently they were going to have to convince her that she needed rescuing. This Ramon Ortega had to be a pretty cagey fellow to have such a woman so firmly convinced.

"Did you tell your father in that letter you wrote that you were going to get married?" Hawke pressed.

Erin paused. "No, no as a matter of fact I didn't. I just told him I was all right and not to worry. Ramon thought it would be better if we didn't tell him about the rest until after we're married. What difference does that make?"

Hawke was suddenly grateful to whatever instinct it was that had caused him to carry the folded-up ransom note and small ring Marshal Cook had passed him in the saloon. He dug inside his jacket pocket and handed the note to Erin.

There was no denying that the soiled and much-creased note was written in Ramon's hand. The demand for money was there, and the threat. The threat that if his demands were not met, he would cut off Erin's finger and send it along after the ring he had included with the note.

The words leaped up off the sheet of paper at her, and Erin stiffened, her mouth going dry. "The ring?" she asked, already knowing, and at the same time fearing the answer.

Hawke brought the ring out of his pocket, handing it to her without a word.

It twinkled there, laying in the palm of her hand in the lamplight. "I thought I had lost it somewhere," she mused quietly. For a moment in the soft light she looked like a hurt little girl, then she turned her gaze on Hawke, expression changing, eyes icing over.

"He used me!" she exploded as the truth she had chosen to ignore broke blindingly over her. His love had been a sham. However, if the truth be known, she had half guessed that fact from the beginning, but had been too busy running from a too-pompous and overbearing father to recognize what had been before her eyes. "Why, that miserable, belly-crawling, backbiting bastard used me!"

At her choice of very descriptive words Hawke flinched, though they certainly seemed to fit. He had never heard a woman use the term before, except in saloons or maybe the red-light district of a cow town.

Erin Keller was by turns appalled, indignant, and a spitting wildcat, a string of profanity issuing from her fair lips that she could have only picked up in the railroad camps of the men who laid rails. The profanity would have curled the hair of the man who called her daughter.

"I'll kill him," Erin ended breathlessly. "I'll kill him!"

"You can't," Ringo protested. "We have to rescue you. We made a deal. Get five thousand and amnesty when we bring you back."

"Do you want me to tell you what you can do with your amnesty for all I care?" Erin threatened, brown eyes wild.

"We're not really interested," Hawke replied evenly, attempting to take hold of the situation. He was now certain he could hear the drone of the motorcycles in the distance. They were coming back. "We have to get out of here in one hell of a hurry, and if we have to, we'll take you out of here by force." Hawke stood tall above her, the black of his clothes accenting his towering build. His square face was stern, thin lips compressed tightly in what he hoped was a firm line.

"You just try it," Erin snapped, "and I'll scream this place down around all your ears. Ramon's Yaqui guards shouldn't be too far from here looking for you anyway."

Hawke stared hard at her, trying to read whether she was bluffing, decided she was not, but knew they would have to take the risk anyway. The simple word Yaqui had turned Ringo pale, and the distant drone of the approaching cycles was growing louder. Everyone in the room was aware of it now.

"We'll have to take that chance," Hawke said icily, reaching snake fast to grab her slim shoulders before she could turn away. "I'll give you one more chance. We're running out of time. Do you go like this," he glanced down at the flimsy nightgown, "or do you change clothes and come with us?"

Feeling the viselike grip of Hawke's fingers biting firmly into her shoulders, Erin backpedaled a bit. "We're all adults," she pleaded. "Surely we can talk about this."

Authoritatively Hawke spun her around, giving her a light push in the direction of the wardrobe. "No time. We'll talk later."

Erin paused. "But . . ."

"Ma'am,"—Hawke pointed out impatiently—"we're all standing in *his* bedroom and he's not likely to be gone too long."

Snatching a split skirt and blouse from the wardrobe, Erin started to angrily jerk them on behind the cover of a screen after she slipped out of the nightgown, the one Ramon had so favored. Better to be dressed no matter which way things went. "Then we'd better settle matters quickly," Erin replied to Hawke's statement.

Hawke sighed.

"You really want to kill him?" Ringo asked, dumfounded by a pretty woman's desires in that direction. "Yourself?"

"Well, maybe not kill," Erin admitted as she stepped around the screen clothed in brown riding skirt, tan shirt, knee-high brown leather boots, and a broad brown leather belt into which she had tucked a small pistol. "But you don't understand. He *used* me. I want him to pay." She half turned toward Hawke as to seek understanding from that quarter. "When I first came here I hadn't . . . I mean, I wasn't . . . I mean, before that I never . . . well, you know! And he *used* me!"

Standing right there in the bedroom she had shared with Ramon Ortega, Hawke squirmed uncomfortably at the confession. Cupping her elbow in his hand, he started to steer her toward the door.

"The best way you can get back at him is to get yourself clear of here so he can't collect the ransom. And let's all of us clear out of here so none of us gets killed."

Erin stopped so abruptly Hawke nearly tripped over her rigid stance. "That's not enough!"

"It's enough for me," Ringo interjected.

"Look, Erin, Miss Keller"—Hawke used his most persuasive voice—"if we don't get ourselves out of here right now," he spoke a little louder over the roar of the thundering Indians as Jackson and Pronto approached the front gates, "nobody is going to have much of a chance to do anything. We have to get clear of his home ground, out in the open where we can draw him out. I've got more men out there and in about two minutes they're going to go riding straight into those Yaquis of yours."

"They're not *my* Yaqui," Erin snapped, "but all right, let's go. He'll come after me all right."

That was exactly what Hawke was afraid of. Shadowing her to the door, Hawke slipped past and led the way out.

CHAPTER 14

Outside, with Erin in tow, holding her firmly by one slim, pulsing wrist, Salvador Hawke decided that Jackson's and Pronto's timing was not so bad after all. He, Rawlins, and Ringo could see the flitting, shadowy forms of the guards Erin had spoken of heading for the front gates at the approaching roar. From the shelter of the adobe's shadowed doorway, Hawke paused to let his eyes adjust from the yellow light of the lamplit room to the silvery light of the moon. For the moment the way was clear to the motorcycles and Rawlins' horse. They seemed undisturbed and for a fleeting instant it occurred to Hawke that the Yaqui guards might ambush them there. But then it became evident that the roar of the additional approaching machines had drawn them off.

As a sidewinder slithering across the open desert, Hawke led the way, pulling Erin along, followed in tight formation by Ringo and Rawlins.

Every muscle tensed in his body, Hawke paused as Rawlins swung with deceptive ease up into the saddle and Ringo straddled his machine. "Wait till I start the machine, then hop on," Hawke advised Erin as he released his grip on her wrist and threw a leg over the Indian.

Erin looked extremely nervous at the whole idea. "I think I'd rather ride with him," she whispered, jerking her thumb in Rawlins' direction.

"What's the matter, ain't you ever seen a motorcycle before?" Hawke hissed back. "Not even with all the traveling you've done to Chicago and the like?"

"Oh I've seen them all right," Erin admitted. "I just don't think this is the place for them." For a few horrible seconds Erin had a vision of their trying to draw Ramon Ortega out after them and that damn machine coming up with a flat tire in the middle of a lonesome stretch of desert.

"Forget it," Hawke returned sharply. "He's heading in a different direction and you're riding with me." Hawke did not give her any more room for argument. With no wasted motion he turned the engine over, bringing it to a fine roar as Ringo followed suit. "Get on," he ordered.

Erin glanced longingly over her shoulder in Rawlins' direction as the man lifted his mount to an easy lope, exiting through the back gate as the Yaqui turned from the front wall at the twin roars from behind them. There was no time now to debate it. Swinging a leg over the machine, Erin sat up tight behind Hawke, wrapping strong arms about his middle for support. She could feel the rock hardness of his muscles beneath her arms as he kicked the machine forward, rolling for the front gate.

Cringing, Erin tried to make herself smaller behind Hawke's body. She could tell Hawke did not plan on attempting a backdoor exit like his man Rawlins. As she hung on for dear life, Erin mumbled a little prayer she had not used since childhood. Just a few hours ago she would have sworn the Yaqui would not shoot just because she was on the machine behind Hawke. But the Yaqui guards were a strange bunch anyway, and now in the light of what she had learned about Ramon Ortega, it would be hard to tell what the Indians' orders would be concerning her attempting to leave without him.

Her instant evaluation of her situation proved accurate as they whipped through the gates, gathering speed while gunshots popped around them at close range. She was thankful that the Yaqui did not know enough to aim at the tires. That was something Ramon would think of. In the past Erin had been known to change her mind quickly, and this was one of those times. Suddenly her plan for revenge seemed not so very important when viewed in the newly dawning light of her knowledge. Just eluding Ramon's long-reaching grasp could prove to be an arduous undertaking. Clamping her teeth tightly closed, she buried her face in Hawke's shoulder, shielding her face against the wind as a loud roaring informed her of the other two cycles joining them.

Erin heard hoofbeats behind them. It had to be her imagination, because above the roar of the four engines she would not be able to hear a thing. But she knew that the horses were coming. With nothing at the fort to guard while Ramon Ortega was gone, they would be coming after them. And they would be joining up with Ramon and the rest of his men. All of them rode powerful horses. It was something Ramon had always made sure of. And there were the Yaqui. They had always made Erin nervous, those hard, expressionless faces staring at her, through her, when they chanced to set eyes on her. Even though things had quieted down considerably since the days when the Yaqui were the scourge of Mexico, stories about their escapades still persisted. His men, Ramon had always assured her, were civilized and, besides, most of them were half Mexican, not that Erin had ever been able to figure out what difference that would make considering they had been raised traditional Yaqui. The only real difference was the fact that their mothers had been stolen from Mexican villages years before.

The ride on the motorcycle was far from smooth, and before long Erin's thoughts turned more to the ache in her back and in her arms as she clung to the powerful man in front of her to keep from tumbling off the back of the machine. As time dragged slowly by she wished even more strongly that she was astride a powerful horse instead of on the jarring, deafening machine.

They cut through the copse of trees, swung wide, skirting a couple of sandy hills and bore into a fiercely northerly direction. They could not travel as fast as Hawke would have liked, the darkness both benefiting and hampering them. It lent them cover, but it slowed their progress. The motorcycles had formed a pattern when they had rejoined their forces, putting Jackson at his left flank, Ringo at his right, and Pronto behind and slightly to one side to avoid the pebbles and dust. The engines throbbed almost in rhythm, and Hawke doubted they were going to have to resort to any fancy maneuvers. It would be just a wild dash

for the border and Coyote Springs, where Marshal Cook would
be waiting for them. Hawke did not care what high-and-mighty
Miss Erin Keller wanted. Revenge or no, they were not going to
stop to let Ramon Ortega and his *banditos* catch up with them.

Salvador Hawke kept his eyes rigidly straight ahead, but he
was acutely aware of the soft, warm, womanly presence at his
back. He could not ignore her pressed up tight against him,
hanging on tight. With an effort Hawke switched his thoughts to
her attitude, focusing out her warmth so close to him. She was as
bad as Rawlins, taking one look at the machines and declaring
she wanted to ride with him. And her with a railroad man for a
daddy to boot. If anyone should understand and appreciate
progress, it should be her.

They were not nearly as far from the strange bandit fortress
east of Casas Grandes as Hawke thought when Jackson waved a
frantic signal as he pulled up level alongside, gesturing wildly to
the north, a little off center of dead ahead. A string of riders
were heading in their direction. Hawke counted at least ten; it
was difficult to be able to be really accurate at that distance.
From beside him, Hawke could read Jackson's sign talk. It was
Ramon Ortega and his bandits. Somehow Hawke and his men
had altered course, and now they were doubling back on them.
Hawke set his jaw but he was not really concerned. The Yaqui
had been left a goodly distance behind. They would just have to
circle Ortega and outrun him. This was strange country and in
the dark Hawke was a bit unsure of himself, but the horses
would also be slowed, and the noise the machines made had
served them well in the past.

The river was a couple of miles west of them. They were running a course roughly parallel to it, but there would come a
time, soon, when they would have to cross it again. Hawke was
not looking forward to it. They had to be able to cross at
Hawke's time and in Hawke's way. Now was not the time. He
could not risk a motorcycle upset in the water.

Hills dropping away behind them for the time being, the flats
opened up before them. More hills and mountains lay in the distance and to their side, their peaks a blacker black than the
night that framed them. For the moment they were out in the

open, and Salvador Hawke preferred it that way. He glanced at the galloping horses strung out before them, then hung his head briefly over his shoulder.

"Hang on!" he shouted to Erin above the roaring of the combined motors.

In spite of muscles strained and tired, Erin tightened her grip about his waist and squeezed her eyes tightly shut. No matter how it turned out, she did not want to see it.

Hawke hunched forward on his machine, gunned the motor, and let it spurt forward beneath his experienced hand. Something in the set of the riders on horseback, the way they handled their mounts with one hand, told Hawke they had their guns out. But, Hawke convinced himself, no one had ever been a crack shot in the dark. Not even the dark touched by silvery illuminations of a partial moon. Hawke felt the constricting grip of Erin Keller's arms wrapped around his lower chest. Considering he was riding point, he wished she was up behind one of the other men, but things were as they were. For the moment there was no changing them. He was the most experienced rider, and taking her up behind him had been almost reflex.

As the motorcycles surged in their direction the horses panicked. But their panic was not nearly so extreme as the horses ridden by the detectives, nor were they as uncontrollable. Hawke swore as they drew nearer, the outlines of the individual men separating themselves from the blurs of the horses they rode. The animals had their ears pricked forward, heads held high, tossing them with agitation, forefeet lifting and touching the earth again nervously as if in a shuffling prance, but they were going to stand. It was not possible. Hawke gave an ear-piercing yell and waved his men off, swerving abruptly away from a head-on collision less than twenty-five yards from where the riders were strung out in a sparse line across their path.

The machines cut sharply to the right, Hawke keeping the river firmly in mind, not believing it would be possible for Ortega and his men to push the horses that far, but not taking any chances either. Better the mountains that rose up to the east than the river to the west.

Before them the horses swung around just as sharply, as if on a military maneuver, and gunshots cracked through the suddenly heavy air. Bullets whipped past close enough to give Hawke cause to re-evaluate his stand on night shooting. Ramon Ortega and his pack were like a band of guerrilla fighters moving with disciplined precision that was going to bring their animals closer than Hawke liked to think about as they completed the turn that was supposed to have circled the bandits on the open flats with comparative ease.

It was too dark to see the open land that lay sprawled before them to pick out the occasional, unexpected clump of low cactus or odd cluster of rocks. Only one clear-cut choice was open to them, and Hawke took it without hesitation. With a sharp motion he opened the throttle all the way and felt the machine vibrating beneath him nearly leap from between his legs. At the same instant he fell the sharp tug at his midsection as Erin was almost torn off the back, and a heartbeat behind, Ringo, Jackson, and Pronto followed his example. The roar of the combined Indians rose to a screaming pitch, and dust billowed up in a thickening cloud.

Shots rang out in a second volley as the machines skirted the hard-running horses, the vibrating drum of their hoofbeats blending with the screaming roar of the Indians. It was going to be close. Even with the added speed, the risk, it was going to be close. Hawke hunched low over the handlebars, flinching for Erin's exposed back as he completed the wide turn and shot past the lead horseman, cutting so close Hawke could have sworn he could pick out the man's features as he snarled down from the plunging horse's back. Had he actually seen the heavy black mustache framing a thick upper lip, eyes small and close-set, the cynical grin that had flashed at their moment of passing, or had it had all been his imagination?

Leaning with the swing of the turning machine, Hawke felt something cold coiling in the pit of his belly, some sixth sense tingling a warning along his limbs as the hoofbeats fell farther behind and another volley of shots pursued them. Hawke glanced to either side. They were all still one, Ringo, Jackson, and Pronto clinging to his shirttails like mud to a woman's petticoats. There was no doubt of Erin's presence—her grip was nearly cutting off his breath, and she was coughing uncontrollably in the thick dust. On impulse Hawke veered suddenly westward, toward the distant river. A bullet snapped near his head; he felt Erin flinch at the closeness of it. Another kicked up dirt somewhere out of his sight, and a third whanged off something with unnerving accuracy. Then, suddenly, they were clear, out of range.

Hawke throttled back just a little, letting out a long sigh of relief. They could outrun them now; slowing down would cut the risk of a spill. The frantic scream of the engine settled down to an even, throbbing roar. Hawke's fine ear seemed to detect a rough coughing sound from nearby, but nothing happened and they pressed on, knifing into the gray skyline that promised the morning sun.

Dawn had barely made its glowing debut, sending brilliant shafts of golden light cascading over the shoulders of the nearing mountains when Hawke signaled a rest stop and shut down his machine. He fought down an impulse to pat his machine as he would a faithful mount that had just pulled more than his share. The Indians, Hawke decided, was the best idea he had ever come up with. Ramon Ortega and his pack of cutthroats were several hours behind, and in Hawke's estimation that put them in the clear from that quarter. Up ahead there could still be trouble from the railroad detectives—that is, if they had had the sand it took to get fresh mounts and start down into Mexico after them. Considering there was only water in so many places in the desert, it was possible they would be running into them again. This time, though, they would have the kidnaped daughter of the railroad's head honcho with them. And there was Coyote Springs where the marshal would be waiting.

When Hawke shut down the Indian, Erin Keller climbed off the back, feeling stiff as fried fat and about as brittle. She felt as if every muscle and joint in her body were on fire and she had been hit across the middle of her back with a broad board. But she had not complained and she would not. The gauntlet of the night before was emblazoned on her mind with the glowing colors of a nightmare. The dark, ghostly figures on horseback towering above them, for an instant close enough to smell the sweat of the horses. The noise. The snap of the gunshots, sharp and ear-splitting even above the roar of the damned machines. If she got out of this alive Erin swore she would never get within a block of one of those machines again as long as she lived.

Hart Jackson, a man Erin had recognized immediately as being at least part Indian, took advantage of the stop to trail out on foot to the next ridge, scouting ahead. For his presence Erin was grateful. She did not feel the need of any more surprises.

Exhausted, Erin dropped to sit on the hard earth, cross-legged, while Hawke stooped to start a fire.

"Time for some coffee and jerky if you're a mind," Hawke presented the news offhandedly, as if it were not really important.

Erin resented his attitude. At that moment she would have bartered her heart and soul for a strong, black cup of coffee. After the harrowing ride she was thoroughly disgruntled and not even sure her stomach was ready for the tough beef jerky he offered, but she knew she had to try to eat it. There was no telling what this maniac had in mind for them next. It could be a long time between meals as long as she rode with him.

After the coffee had brewed Hawke handed Erin a cup of the steaming brew and sat back on his heels with a cup of his own, gazing at her from narrowed eyes. In spite of her bad temper she was really something to see. That railroad man had done himself proud in his daughter. She, Hawke decided, had to be about the only decent thing the man had ever produced. It was damn hard to associate her with the railroad in any remote attachment. She looked like an angel, and while she had opened those soft, full lips to swear like a fishwife back there in Ortega's camp, it had done nothing to detract from her as far as he was concerned. And from the moment he had first seen her clearly back there in that room, she did something to him that he was not ready to admit. Hawke tried to put the erotic thoughts from his mind. Though he was sure they had come through the worst of it there could yet be trouble ahead. His mind had to be clear, he had to be ready. Bandits prowled the border like scavengers waiting to pick some unwary traveler's bones clean, and distractions were not what he needed now.

Erin was returning Hawke's stare with the same intensity. Suddenly her catlike brown eyes narrowed. "You haven't even told me your name."

Hawke grinned. "Wasn't much time, as I recall. It's Hawke, Salvador Hawke." He gestured to the others one at a time. "Ringo, Hart Jackson scouting the ridge up ahead, and Pronto."

"Salvador?" Erin's expression was quizzical, not doubting, just surprised.

Hawke shrugged. "It's what my ma stuck me with. Hawke is what I go by."

"In this country I can see why," Erin observed, grinning around the rim of her cup as she took another sip.

Surprisingly, Erin felt herself begin to relax in Hawke's company. Maybe it was just the coffee. "What about the other one?" she asked. "The one with the horse."

"That was George Rawlins," Hawke told her easily, finding the talk welcome, her voice soothing as his eyes skipped around the camp, watching everything with a wary eye, especially Pronto and Ringo as they poked around one of the machines. "He doesn't care much for the twentieth century."

Erin laughed, the sound of it drifting over the short distance between then like the whisper of the wind. "Can't say I blame him." Erin glanced around as if becoming fully aware of her surroundings for the first time. "How long are we going to stay here?"

"Just long enough to eat and rest a bit," Hawke answered. "You could stretch out on the ground for a while, maybe catch a couple'a winks."

"No, thank you, I'm all right." Erin continued to sip the coffee, taking an occasional nibble of the jerky she held in one curled hand. "You do like the twentieth century?"

Hawke shrugged. "It's not a question of liking it, it's a question of a man knowing when to change and when to accept change. Those machines are just a small part of it. A man changes or he gets run over by everyone else who does."

"True," Erin agreed. "But it makes you sound more like a businessman than a train robber. And sometimes a man can embrace change too quickly. Sometimes a change like those motorcycles can be incongruous with where a man puts them to use."

Hart Jackson was still up on the ridge, Pronto and Ringo were still fooling around by the machines. For an instant Salvador Hawke looked blank, then from the depths of his memory he dredged up the meaning of the word she had thrown at him. "Not those machines," Hawke returned firmly as he squinted in Ringo and Pronto's direction. Was he mistaken or was there a wet stain on the ground beside Pronto's Indian?

Erin shrugged and abruptly changed the subject. "Why did you rob all those trains? I was on one, you know. I saw you. I guess it was before you got those machines of yours, back near the Colorado border. I was going to Santa Fe to my father. Caused an awful lot of trouble when you stole the engine, leaving all of us out there in the middle of nowhere. It was two days before they got another engine up there to pull the train."

Hawke could not suppress a grin. That was where he had seen her before, the face in the window of the passenger car the last time they had robbed a train with their horses. The time they had slipped away by the merest thread of good fortune. "Those are the risks you take riding the rails," he said philosophically.

"But what about the trains? Why do you rob them?"

"A debt I owed. Why did you run off with that cutthroat Ortega?"

"I didn't know he was a cutthroat," Erin protested. "Besides, I thought I loved him."

"You don't?"

"How could I love a cutthroat, bandit, and worse?" Erin was indignant at the suggestion.

It was tough to understand women, Hawke decided, especially ones like Erin Keller. He continued to squint past her to where Ringo and Pronto remained intent on the Indian they had singled out for their attention, Pronto's machine. All the attention the machine was getting was beginning to make Hawke nervous. As much as he was enjoying the quiet break he was sharing with Erin, he knew he'd better get himself over there.

"Excuse me." Hawke offered his most mannerly side, then rose and started with long, purposeful strides in the direction of the machine and the two men.

Climbing to her feet, Erin walked right along behind him. This whole situation concerned her welfare, and she was not going to be left out of anything.

Hart Jackson had abandoned the ridge and was headed their way with an even, swinging walk when Hawke reached the scene of the huddled conference.

"What the hell's going on now?" Hawke demanded, unaware of Erin following him until she popped up close beside him, face set in concerned lines.

Ringo shook his head and gazed at the machine, pointing to the wet stain that had spread beneath it.

Elbowing his way closer to the machine, Hawke caught the first whiff of gas fumes floating on the air and recognized the wet spot for what it was. The Indian's lifeblood spilled into the earth.

"See anything?" Hawke asked over his shoulder of Jackson without even looking his way, too intent on the damage sustained by the machine to divert his attention.

"No," Jackson replied. "All clear for now. What happened?"

"Can't tell exactly yet," Hawke replied, "but we're going to find out." He began to roll up his sleeves doctorlike, probing a finger into the mechanism's innards. "Keep a lookout, Hart. Give us a warning if trouble shows. I'm going to make this baby run again." Hawke's voice rang with determination and self-confidence.

Hart Jackson nodded briefly and lit out to the south at a dog trot. Hawke bent to his task and Erin sat back to wait. She had an uneasy feeling about the situation, but now was not the time to voice it.

After six hours Hawke was no further ahead fixing the machine than in the first six minutes after he had started. It was six hours spent mostly coming to terms with the inevitable. When he unkinked his body and stood up, shirtless, sweat glistening in beads across his furred chest, he felt years older. He had failed. There was no way to plug the hole in the fuel tank, or to repair the damage to the other parts the bullet had clipped when it had hit. He had vainly tried to start the machine a couple of times in spite of the certain knowledge that it would not start, but all it had done was cough once or twice pitifully, as if choking on the few remaining drops of fuel that puddled the bottom of the tank, wheeze like a consumptive, and fall silent again. Even had he gotten it started, it slowly dawned on Hawke that they would not have the fuel needed to replace what had been lost. Upon checking the other tanks, he wondered whether or not they would even have enough fuel to get to Coyote Springs as it was.

"No way to plug that hole," Hawke announced, sitting on the ground slumped in defeat.

"You can't fix it?" Pronto demanded. "Ain't nothin' you can plug that hole with?!"

"Not unless you want Ringo to ride alongside real close with his finger stuck in it," Hawke snapped, angered at his inability to do anything.

Erin laid a comforting hand on Hawke's shoulder, surprised at herself that she did. She should be just as upset as Pronto, even more so. If Ramon Ortega caught up with her now . . . She had seen examples of his temper directed at others and had no desire to see it turned in her direction.

Hart Jackson dog-trotted into camp, an anxious expression twisting his features. "That thing fixed yet?"

Hawke shook his head. "You see something?"

"Whole passel of riders coming up hard from the south," Jackson laid it out fast. "Don't see how it could be anybody but Ortega and his bunch."

Hawke swore. "We're leaving!" In an instant he changed from defeated motorcycle repairman to strong leader. "Pronto, you're riding double with Ringo now." He snapped out the order.

Pronto swore under his breath, glancing heavenward in his agitation.

"Let's move!" Hawke bellowed. His words echoed with the power of command.

CHAPTER 15

Hawke felt a bit stiff from sitting crouched up close to the disabled machine for so long, but the throb of the cycle pulsating beneath him, and Erin's arms wrapped around him, clinging, relaxed him somehow while the threat of impending danger sent the blood singing through his veins. It had been a long time since he had felt so alive. It kept a man young when he had to be on his toes every minute, when he never knew which direction trouble was coming from next. Maybe, if the truth be known, that had been the root of all their recent troubles, when things had started going wrong for them. Maybe everything had gotten too easy and they had relaxed. Maybe this was what they needed to bring them to life again.

Jackson ranged a bit ahead, cresting the hills and ridges, sweeping down the narrow valleys and washes, clearing the way before them. Behind, Ortega's riders were close, sending a prickle along Hawke's spine. Jackson was the only one riding single now. Hawke carried Erin behind, and Ringo and Pronto were having their difficulties in adjusting to sharing the same machine. Their progress was considerably slowed, but they had what Hawke believed to be a comfortable margin over the horsemen, and the gap was slowly widening again. Horses had to rest; machines did not. Once again Hawke's foresight was proving sound. The sheer stamina of the machines was what was going to bring them out on top. The only obstacle between them and the border was the Casas Grandes River. They had forded it once and it did not seem such a monumental undertaking to ford it a second time. Their course was drifting westerly now; they would reach the river before sundown.

In spite of Erin's warm softness pressed up behind his back, her breath warm and gusty against his cheek when she tried to speak to him above the roar of the machine, Rawlins came to Hawke's mind. The man was alone, on horseback. Hawke hoped none of Ortega's bunch had taken out after him. At the moment Rawlins was one up on him. He had saved his bacon back there at Ortega's fort when he had cold-cocked the guard. Hawke wanted a chance to bring things back to even again.

Up ahead on a brown and dusty hill Jackson appeared, pulling his motorcycle to a stop and motioning for them to come on. Hawke squinted into the bright sunlight, gazing steadily at Jackson. Something about the way he sat the machine, the way he held himself, spoke of trouble.

Hawke gunned his machine to take the steep hill with its double burden as Erin behind him leaned forward, shifting her weight with the machine, moving with him. It made it difficult to keep his mind on important matters.

"Riders to the north," Jackson barked as Hawke drew up alongside, clinging to the hill's steep grade. "Three of 'em."

One leg braced on the downhill side and one on the uphill, Hawke frowned. Those damned detectives never quit. And Hawke was only too aware that they had not earned their amnesty yet. Marshal Cook's warning still rang in his ears. They were fair game until Erin was returned.

"Which side of the river?" Hawke asked, remembering the trees and rocks on the west side that marked the river's ford.

"This side."

"How far to the ford? Can we make it ahead of them?"

Jackson shrugged and gestured behind him, beyond the crest of the hill he was braced against. "Ford's right over there." He left something unsaid, words hanging unspoken on the air like unwashed dirty laundry.

Cresting the hill, Hawke put down a foot on either side of his machine to brace himself and looked out over the hard reality Jackson had not put into words. Below, the Casas Grandes River flowed in a broad ribbon from the north to the south, its waters glittering beneath the desert sun. The same river they had crossed, knifing deeper into Mexico, but not the same. It was broader, deeper, and moving more swiftly, its surface rippled, and in places, frothy. Only two days before they had been at this same ford and the river had been no more than a swiftly flowing creek. During that short time something had happened. Snow melting in the high country and gathering in small rivulets and creeks, building until it reached this river, maybe a cloudburst fifty miles away, or maybe too many people spit in the river once too often. Hawke did not pretend to understand the intricacies of Mother Nature. Whatever the reason, the river was at some stage of flood, and there was no telling what stage. The river could be either rising or receding. And they did not have the time to wait it out. Ortega and his bunch of cutthroats were not very far behind, and the railroad's trio of Fisher, Barnett, and West were even closer.

"Any other ford near here?" Hawke yelled into Jackson's ear above the rumbling idle of the three machines and the rush of the water below.

Jackson shook his head negatively. "North it would get worse. South there might be a way, but there's no way to be sure, and that would put us deeper in Mexico again."

Hawke eyed the ford. "Think we can make it across?" He was a little worried with double weight on two of the Indians.

Jackson shrugged evasively. "No tellin' how deep the middle is."

Swearing under his breath, Hawke eyed the swiftly flowing river. A rising cloud of dust billowed to the north above swiftly moving specks.

"Ohmigod! Look!" Erin cried, directing their attention behind and to the east of them where more dust rose skyward from beneath the hoofs of plainly laboring mounts.

Ortega had to have signaled ahead to have riders there.

There was no choice. They had to cross, and they had to cross here. Jackson was the only one straddling his machine alone. He would have to try to ford the river first. They would take their cue from him.

As if reading Hawke's thoughts, Jackson let his machine roll, taking the steep grade of the hill at a sideways slant and pausing at the bottom, sizing up the situation before easing his machine forward once again. He slid into the water slick as a hot knife through butter, angling slightly into the flow as the machine sank deeper and deeper into the water. He held the machine to a steady pace, letting the water part broadside along him, the Indian's motor suspended bare inches above the surface. With the apparent ease of a fish, Jackson continued to knife his motorcycle through the water as it began to fall away from him and the tires strove to get a fresh grasp in the sifting silt of the shallows.

On the far side of the river Hart Jackson emerged, gunning the cycle's engine in victory. He cut a tight circle in the dirt well above the high-water line, then swept in a wide arch to the towering cottonwoods that edged the far side to await the others.

Hawke still did not possess an overabundance of confidence. But he kicked his machine off, following in Jackson's tracks down the side of the hill, pausing before the river, listening to the steady throb of Ringo's machine behind, glancing once more at the dust clouds that were rapidly closing on them. Then he started forward, slowly. Ringo, his ears told him, was no more than a machine length behind. It would have been better had he not trailed along so closely, but there was no time to stop to have a discussion about it. Hawke kept his machine moving, feeling the strong pull beneath, feeling the strangulation hold Erin had adopted when they entered the water. He did not want to contemplate what significance that grip had, he only wanted to be across and clear of the lapping water that rose quickly above their feet and up along their legs, covering half the tires easily and reaching hungrily for more. Erin was silent, but Hawke was aware of the increased cadence of her breathing and suspected her eyes were squeezed tightly shut.

Sitting the motorcycle stiff as the first time he had ridden one, Hawke was aware of the strange spongy, sinking sensation that crept up the motorcycle and entered his limbs. His belly felt cold, as if it were about to drop around his knees, but still the machine kept on, narrow tires seeking a purchase in the shifting river bottom with a steady defiance of the powerful, driving force of the water sweeping and surging against them. The river was much broader than it was deep, a fact for which Hawke was about to give proper thanks when it happened.

From behind Hawke heard a pained cry and glanced back to see a thick fold of Erin's riding skirt caught in the spokes of the Indian's rear wheel where the swiftly flowing water had swept it. Her leg jerked sharply backward and against the spinning wheel had brought a yelp of pain and surprise from her lips.

Instantly, Hawke stopped his machine, and in the same instant felt it begin to sink, caught in the grip of the river's silty bottom.

"Tear it free!" Hawke yelled over his shoulder to Erin, who was already frantically tugging at the soddenly snared knot of cloth without success.

"I can't!" Erin wailed, feeling the steady sinking of the machine beneath her.

Hawke was off the machine in a flash, braced against the swiftly flowing water that threatened to sweep him from his feet with each sinking step that took him deeper into the silt bottom. With his weight removed, the machine commenced to sink a little more slowly, buying some time as Ringo pulled his machine alongside, stopping to help.

"Get that thing moving!" Hawke bellowed once he realized what Ringo had done, but it was already too late. The machine, caught in the sucking river bottom, had begun to sink at a rapid rate beneath even heavier weight than Hawke's machine had carried.

"Climb off and drag it out of there!" Hawke commanded as the water reached up the idling engine and killed it with a bubbling splutter while Hawke bent over Erin's caught skirt.

"I'm going to drown!" Erin moaned, ceasing to tug at the wadded material when Hawke slapped her hand away and the river's water claimed his machine as it had Ringo's. The water snuffed the laboring engine with no effort as he continued to jerk at the stubborn knot of cloth wrapped in the spokes.

The machine was still sinking inexorably into the river bottom's depth, though much slower now, while Ringo and Pronto, hip deep in flooding river, struggled to extricate the machine they had ridden on as Hawke moved around the motorcycle, on which Erin was still sitting, to the downriver side. With sudden decision and determination, Erin awkwardly tried to climb down off the machine in spite of her impediment.

Braced now, firmly set, Hawke gave a hard jerk on the cloth as Erin started to clamber off. The cloth gave suddenly beneath the power of Hawke's assault, snapping free and jerking hard against Erin as she was caught in midair of her dismount, the momentum snapping her forward as if she had been launched from a slingshot. She hit the water in a headlong dive upriver against the current and surfaced spluttering, her hair wrapped around her face in a blinding curtain. Hawke grabbed for his machine as it began to topple, one handlebar disappearing beneath the roiling waters before he snagged the other.

"Get your feet under you and stand up!" Hawke shouted instructions to Erin as she surfaced gasping and gagging, blinded by her hair streaming across her face and throat only to be swept over again by the force of the driving water.

Ringo and Pronto, exhausted by their efforts, managed to haul the heavy machine they had ridden clear of the sucking mud and plunging waters as those same waters tumbled Erin again, carrying her swiftly along in its grip.

Erin Keller had never yelled for help before in her life, but finally in this, the matter of survival was taking precedence over pride, and she let out a long, throaty yell.

"Help!" burst on a bubble of air as Erin surfaced long enough to gasp a fresh lungful of air a couple of feet out of Hawke's reach.

Hawke swore lustily. By damn if she was not going to do it. She was going to drown right there in front of his eyes in water hardly over her waist in depth. Relinquishing his hold on the machine, he lunged for her, reaching for her outstretched hand glimmering whitely beneath the surface of the river's dark waters. He swore forcefully at the river, at the law, at the railroads, and even at his mother, who had given birth to him those many years before just so he could end up here, now.

Snagging her wrist, Hawke pulled Erin to him, wrapping his

arm around her waist to support her, and started moving steadily to the far riverbank where his men waited, Jackson striding forward into the shallows to help haul Erin out.

Placing her limp in Jackson's powerful arms, Hawke saw Erin lifted clear of the water and carried out to the bank, then turned his attention to his sunken machine. He managed to locate it again by the distinct ripple one cocked handlebar was still causing in the river's surface. He reached it and started attempting to haul it free of the river's grip when the pounding of hoofbeats jerked him erect.

Instinct made Hawke grab the rifle out of the boot alongside the motorcycle's front wheel. Wet as it was, it was still a rifle, and he was not going to let the river snatch it away from him. Slowed by the swift current and deep, shifting mud beneath his boots, Hawke was still several yards offshore when the first shot sounded. It slapped the water close beside him and sent him into a flat dive beneath the river's icy waters. As he smacked the water his hat left his head and started drifting downstream, but Hawke managed to hang on to the rifle and clawed his way along the river bottom toward the bank. He did not dare to surface again, until with lungs burning and eyes bulging, he broke from the water and made a dash for the trees where Jackson was attempting to lay down a covering fire with the only dry rifle between them. Ringo and Pronto had their six-guns out, but for the moment the horsemen on the far side of the river were out of range.

Gunfire split the air, and bullets stitched a zigzag pattern at Hawke's heels as he ran, legs pumping, and threw himself over the pile of rocks Jackson was shooting from in a free-wheeling somersault that was well beyond control. Piling into Ringo and Pronto, bowling them over, Hawke wound up sprawled in a tangle of arms, legs, and rifle, flat on his back staring up into Erin's river-damp face.

Erin sighed and glared. She had held it in about as long as any mortal could, but now she could stand it no longer. "Well," she finally demanded stridently, "what now?"

Bruised, half drowned, and madder than an old lobo with his paw caught in a wolf trap, Hawke returned her glare, picking himself up and snatching his dripping weapon out of the dirt. "Now . . . I clean my rifle."

CHAPTER 16

Erin wanted to say something more, but she was cut off by a bullet whanging off rock in a ricochet that sent it tearing into the bark of the nearest cottonwood. Instinctively she jerked back, ducking, and beginning to swear again in that railroad lineman's vernacular.

Elbowing his way up beside Jackson, Hawke began feverishly wiping his rifle down. "Who do you think it is?"

Jackson shrugged, aimed another shot at the distant shore where he had forced the horsemen into hiding, and pulled off a clean shot that snapped at an exposed boot heel. "They ain't got much to say. And the woman don't seem to be slowing 'em down none. I reckon it has to be Ortega's bunch."

"How the hell did they get here so fast?" Hawke might have been questioning the air surrounding them.

Jackson answered anyway. "Had to have signaled ahead somehow. They ain't got down to serious shootin' yet so it seems like they're just gonna keep us pinned here till ol' Ortega himself shows up."

"Shouldn't be too long either," Hawke added, working hastily on his rifle.

They were in a pretty pickle. No horses, no room to run, and one machine among the lot of them. That meant two could ride. The situation could come down to drawing straws to determine who would take the Keller woman out. Hawke recoiled at the thought but knew it might have to be faced. Looked like they had really done it this time.

"You boys just throw down your guns and come on out peaceable!" A strange yet vaguely familiar voice rang out across the river separating them. "This is the end of the line. We're taking you in."

Hawke quickly finished what he was doing and began loading the clean, dry weapon.

Erin jerked upright, craning her neck to see over the rocks and yet still keep under cover. "Tom Fisher," she filled in the blank. "One of Daddy's men."

"When the hell did they show up?" Hawke demanded, jacking shells into his rifle as fast as his fingers could work. Pronto was following suit with his own weapon. They were fully armed again, rifles snatched from a watery grave.

"We've got you covered, give yourselves up!" Fisher repeated. "We're taking you in one way or another."

"Do you know him?" Hawke asked, turning to Erin. "You recognized his voice."

Erin nodded quickly. "I've met him once or twice, rode with him on the train for a while."

"Well, call out to him, let him know you're here," Hawke urged, looking for something that would give them an edge.

Before Erin could open her mouth another voice—thick with Mexican accent and finely honed with the edge of authority—split the air. "No, *señor*," the voice called amiably in the direction of where the detective lay in concealment, "they are ours. If you leave now, we will not shoot you. It is fair warning."

"You show yourself and I'll blow you to kingdom come," Hawke bellowed the promise across the water. No one was going to move until he had a better chance to think this thing through.

"Ah"—the accented voice was mellow, almost patient—"so the old cougar still has his claws," he baited. "My men thought they were holding an old cat at bay, waiting for me to come and finish him off, but it is plain they were wrong; there is still some fight left."

"Ortega," Erin whispered. "Ramon." She looked a bit pale, but her jaw was set and firm.

"Call out to Fisher," Hawke reminded her, his voice softening. "There are plenty of guns between you and Ortega."

"Tom Fisher!" Erin called shrilly. "It's Erin Keller. I'm over here."

There was a long pause. Hawke thought it unlikely that they would not know of Erin's disappearance, and he was finally proved correct.

"Hang on, Miss Keller," a rough, guttural voice called back across the water. "We'll get you out of there all right."

"I *am* all right!" Erin snapped back, straining her voice. "Just get Ortega off our backs."

"I am desolate, *querida*," Ortega called back, his voice drifting softly on the breeze of the coming evening before Fisher could bark his reply across the water separating them. "We had such good times together. What have I done to turn you against me so?"

"Ramon, you lying lowlife!" Erin shouted back, forgetting herself, barely beginning to have her say before Ortega interrupted again.

"So, you have learned something I would rather you had not." His voice was a bit more cool, more resolute. "Ah, well, do not worry, everything will turn out for the best." He paused the briefest moment, then added in a silky voice that carried well, "And need I remind you, *querida*, that I was never on your back. You were."

Erin colored, feeling the blush climb her throat and suffuse her face with prickly warmth. "Everything will not turn out for the best!" she shrieked at him as if they were the only two people there, the river separating them a mere inconvenience. She leaped to her feet, starting to climb over the large rocks that protected their position. "It won't ever be all right again until I stick a knife in your liver and twist it until your navel pops, you slimy, self-seeking, son-of-a . . ."

Hawke reached out a free hand, snagged Erin by one ankle, and dragged her back inside the circling protection of the rocks as a bullet slammed off one of the boulders, sending dust and chips flying into the air. Erin screamed. Hawke's one hand held his rifle and the other circled her shoulders tightly, his hand braced against her mouth, cutting off the angry flow of words while one leg was thrown over hers to quiet her frantic squirming and struggling.

"You said about enough!" Hawke admonished her in a commanding whisper. "Half the country knows you're here now, so calm down!"

Erin went limp in his grasp, still angry, but not about to fight the strength of Hawke's grip uselessly.

Erin's shrieks had carried well across the open water. *"Querida,"* the infuriating, egotistical voice called back, *"Querida,* do you wish me to rescue you from your rescuers?"

Abruptly Erin started to struggle in Hawke's grasp again, but he held her fast, and in a few seconds she gave up. However, she made no effort to stem the flow of swear words that tickled Hawke's palm where he held it clamped over her mouth.

A little to the north of the bandits' camp on the river, Tom Fisher heard Erin Keller's shriek with the same clarity. "That does it!" he snapped to the two men accompanying him. "We're going to burn them out, flush them from cover. Taking that girl back will get us a bigger bonus than the rewards on those three, and we'll have them all in one sack."

"What about the *banditos?*" Sam West asked logically. "Doesn't seem to me that they'll be sittin' there on their hands while we're doin' this."

"We've got our rifles, don't we?" Fisher asked confidently. "If they come at us we'll cut 'em down. Now get the stuff you need, sneak over there, and get a good blaze going. Cottonwood burns easy enough."

West nodded agreement, but he was not sure this was the wisest thing he had ever done. Tom Fisher might figure himself to be superior to just about everything born or grown, but a man could get himself just as dead from a dumb lucky shot as from an expert marksman. And West had a funny feeling about this. There was more out there than those four outlaws, the girl, and a bunch of bumbling Mexican *banditos* trailing along behind. Still, the money looked mighty good, and Erin Keller's daddy would be properly grateful for the return of his little girl. He would have to be very careful. Sam West was one man who planned on keeping his hide whole.

Ramon Ortega sat on the blind side of a hill, watching the sun dip behind the western hills, sending up its final glow of daylight before fading into the gray-black of early dusk. A man's vision was at its worst at that time of the day, but Ortega's mind seemed to function at its best. He signaled one of his Yaquis to him and indicated the shadows of the trees on the far side of the river.

"I want a fire," Ortega commanded. "I want to burn them out, bring them out into the open." The setting of the sun seemed to precipitate a rash of gunfire, but Ortega ignored it, focusing on his plans. He was out of range; he had chosen his spot carefully.

"Send a man to scout the camp of those north of us," Ortega added. "I want to know how many of them there are and how well they are armed."

The Yaqui nodded, disappearing into the coming night as a shadow passed across the moon.

"They're up to something," Hawke said uneasily, still keeping his grasp on Erin firm, hoping she would settle down before he was forced to turn her loose and grab for his rifle. Hawke could smell real trouble coming, like the scent of rain carrying on the wind.

Jackson nodded in sage agreement. "Seen some shadows slippin' around over there on the far bank. No tellin' what they're chewin' on over there."

Hawke was thinking fast. It was getting dark quickly and they were going to have to do something soon. Their position had been held by the sheltering trees and rocks, but now that the darkness of night was settling in to provide cover for Ortega and his Yaqui scouts as well as the detectives who occupied the far side of the river, the advantage would shift. Ortega would be aware of the same facts. If they didn't do something and do it fast, the whole thing would go down the chutes with nothing gained. Erin, at least, had to be gotten clear of the battleground.

Only one of the machines still functioned. The faithful machines, the dependable machines Hawke had touted from the beginning as the things that could get them there and back no matter what, comparing them to the ever-unpredictable horses. But for the moment he did not want to dwell on past mistakes. One of them had to take Erin out, and quickly. It had finally come down to the drawing of straws.

Erin had ceased her struggling in his tenacious grasp. She lay quietly against him, eyes burning with anger, her body stiff with impotent rage. Cautiously, Hawke removed his hand from her mouth. She was quiet for a long moment, tongue coming out to lick dry lips, the anger in her eyes not for Hawke.

"Well?" she asked cautiously, all too aware of the grip Hawke maintained on her.

"Are you finished?" Hawke asked sarcastically. "From what Jackson tells me we'd better get you out of here now if we're gonna do it. There's only one machine left and no time. We'll be drawing straws to see who takes you out."

"Not on your life!" Erin returned. "If I leave with one of you, the rest are dead. No one is going to die for me. I won't have it!"

"We're dead anyway!" Hawke fired the words at Erin in rhythm to the shots Jackson and Pronto sent into the hills across the river. "Can't you at least let a man die happy? Just knowing you got clear?"

"No!" she snapped. "Maybe we could get Tom Fisher and his men on your side. They've got to be in the same fix as we are, camped on Ortega's coattails like they are."

"I doubt they're going to want to team up with us," Hawke said dryly, remembering the thorough job they had done a few days earlier of scattering their horses out in the desert. "Besides . . ."

"Uh-oh," Jackson cut him off. "Looks like they settled on something to do." He snapped off a couple of shots in the direction of the flickering lights he had indicated, drawing a couple of near misses for his trouble.

"Fire," Erin whispered. "They're going to burn us out!"

"Fire!" Ringo bellowed before Hawke had a chance to reply to Erin's fearful observation, and there was nothing anticipatory about his tone. As one their heads jerked in his direction.

In among the trees a golden glow, a sunset most unnatural, flickered, danced, and grew, stretching higher with each passing moment. An odd distant rustling grew into a sharpening crackle and the smell of smoke drifted on the night wind.

Hawke swore under his breath as an arrow cut a blazing path across the river to thunk solidly into the tree trunk above his head. He jerked it free, snuffing the flame as others followed. Before the arrows had started coming from Ortega's stronghold he had already known it was too late. Tom Fisher or one of his boys had to be responsible for the fire raging within the trees to the north of them, heading with awesome speed in their direction. It was not reasonable to suppose Ortega had torched the trees to the north, then proceeded to send in the flaming arrows to start the fire that was already growing, growling like an enraged beast of the forest.

Using the pinpoints of light that dotted the opposite shore for targets, Hawke fired from the cover of the rocks, trying to decide what to do next. There was only one thing they could do, but the glow from the blaze would silhouette them in the darkness, setting them up like so many fish in a barrel.

Laying an ear to the ground, Jackson paused as arrows whistled above him and gunshots spit rock dust in a fine filtering film over him.

"Riders," he said to Hawke. "Headed this way and comin' mighty fast."

"Christ! What next?" Hawke muttered in reply, knuckles turning white where they gripped the gun stock. "*Soldados?*"

Jackson shrugged. "Whoever it is, sure is a passel of 'em."

"How many?"

"Hard to tell exactly." Jackson paused, listening again. "Eight, ten maybe."

"What are we going to do?" Erin asked apprehensively.

"We're going to run like hell," Hawke assured her, "and Lord help us if any of them catch us out in the open."

CHAPTER 17

Torching the small stand of cottonwoods had not been difficult for Sam West, but on his return to camp he found more than he had bargained for. Lurking outside the perimiter, just outside the sight of either Fisher or Barnett, were a pair of men. West could not make out much more about them in the darkness, but they had to be part of the bandit band.

Cautiously, keeping an eye on the dim shapes of Tom Fisher and Will Barnett at the same time, West edged up on the pair as they watched intently the nonactivity of his partners. They were so damn close they could almost reach out and touch each other, but Fisher and Barnett still remained unaware.

Pulling his gun, West flipped it, butt facing forward. He was going to take the pair alive. There were a few questions he wished to ask them regarding what they were dealing with farther downstream. West did not like to run on blind faith in his own superiority, as Fisher was often content to do.

The noise of the fire growing behind him, crackling and blazing into a roar, West crept up on the pair. Easing forward, muscles coiled for the spring, he paused, then let go, pouncing with the power of a springing catamount, cold-cocking one before the second had any idea of what was happening. The second, though, reacted like second cousin to a bobcat, rolling to one side at the attack, whirling to fight with the speed of a striking snake. West let his momentum carry him, catching the shadowy figure of a man about the waist, hurling him backward almost into Tom Fisher, who knocked him out, but not before the man let loose with a nerve-splitting shriek that slashed across even the growing roar of the fire and the rush of the flooded river.

Striking a match, West held it near the faces of the fallen men, and then he no longer felt the need to ask questions. "Yaqui," he said curtly. "Fisher, it's time to ride."

Fisher looked almost inclined to agree with him, then something caught his eye.

"They're movin'," he snapped. "Fire flushed them out. Get the horses. We're goin' after them."

At that moment neither West nor Barnett was inclined to argue with him as long as they hit leather on the run.

"What was that?" Erin asked breathlessly as the Indian's gutted-cat shriek faded away into the background roar of the growing fire, leaving the odd, prickly feeling along the back of her neck.

"Yaqui death yell, or war cry," Jackson answered, picking himself up from the rocks, preparing to make a run for it as Hawke had instructed. "Hard to tell which. Use it to warn their friends when they figure they bought the farm."

Erin made a face as Hawke pulled her to her feet. Something was in his hand she had not noticed earlier, a cluster of sticks. Silently he held out his hand to his men. As one at a time each pulled one of the sticks from the bunch, Erin watched in growing horror. Hart Jackson pulled the longest. It was as if they had all known it would turn out that way. Hart was about the best rider, and knew the country as none of the others did.

Unceremoniously, Hawke shoved her down behind Jackson as he mounted the remaining machine and brought it to life. Erin tried to climb back off, but Hawke held her firmly in place until Jackson shoved off, roaring away into the night's darkness as they had agreed, leaving Hawke, Ringo, and Pronto to fend for themselves.

Hawke felt an odd lump of ice in the pit of his stomach, but he was not prepared to give up. Crouched low with legs pumping, he with his two men dashed madly for the questionable cover of the closest hills, the heat of the fire almost scorching against their backs.

The fire roared louder, the trees crackling and popping their distress as the fire consumed their trunks, toppling ancient giants as the flood waters rushed above their roots. Horses' hoofs pounded in the distance behind and in front of them, but vaguely, somewhere in the back of his mind, Hawke realized the motorcycle was not pulling away farther, as it should have been. An arrow tipped with fire whipped past his leg to ignite a clump of grass at Hawke's feet when he paused, bullets nipping the air all around them as they pounded on, depending on their feet alone to get them away, as George Rawlins had predicted they would.

Then, suddenly, he loomed before them. Rawlins, a mass of dark shadow smelling of horse sweat and old leather in the darkness. The horses Jackson had heard approaching. George Rawlins on his horse, holding the rest of their old remuda on lead, saddled and ready, including the pair of wagon horses. Jackson had pulled his motorcycle partway up the next hill, giving the horses plenty of clearance, figuring them to be spooked enough already by the close proximity of the roaring fire. He had recognized Rawlins at first sight in spite of the enfolding darkness.

"Figured by now you might be needing these," Rawlins commented in his old familiar drawl. "They sure got sleek and sassy on that fine grass and water," he commented, as if detectives and bandits alike were not mounted and pounding across the surging river after them, the detectives in the lead.

Neither Hawke, Ringo, nor Pronto had any questions as to where Rawlins had popped up from. They just piled into the saddles and sat down to ride.

Sitting a saddle again after all the weeks straddling a machine was an odd sensation, but horse and rider responded as an unbroken team, seeming to strive to reach the motorized machine that led the way across the darkened countryside. Moonlight washed over them in a silver wave, and to the rear, Hawke could barely make out the running forms of three mounted horses.

Hawke pushed their horses to the limit, thankful now that Rawlins had managed to keep them in such good shape. If the railroad detectives overtook them now there would be hell to pay because Ortega and his pack of bloodthirsty cutthroats would be only minutes behind. Not enough time to forge an alliance with a fanatic such as Tom Fisher.

Erin, though, would make it back to safety, Hawke had seen to that. She and Jackson were well in the lead, with the border and Coyote Springs now within their grasp. If he was true to his word, Marshal Liam Cook would be there waiting. Hawke missed Erin's softness at his back, missed her warmth and the soft way her words brushed against his ear when she would try to speak to him aboard the motorcycle. He missed the silkiness of her hair when the wind caught a stray wisp and sent it whipping alongside his face as he drove.

The constant pounding of hoofbeats behind reminded Hawke of what lay to the rear and he began to hope that Liam Cook had had the foresight to bring along the 5th Cavalry to keep him company while he waited.

Time ceased to exist as they raced for the border, Rawlins smiling vaguely with a confidence Hawke could not muster. They pushed on, Hawke gauging their pace to those coming up behind. When they slowed, he pulled back, giving the horses a chance to rest.

It could not have been much more than a hour before dawn when Hawke spotted the motorcycle ahead, and they were gaining rapidly on it. The familiar roar did not color the predawn air. Hawke knew the worst before they came up on Jackson and Erin, anxiously awaiting their arrival. The machine had run out of fuel.

Hawke did not ask questions. Jackson and Erin swung up on the spare horses they had been rotating with during the long night. With a last, backward, saddened gaze, Hawke led out, the border now no more than an hour away. The last Indian was downed and they were in an all-out run for home.

Dawn was streaking the sky with yellow and pink among the gray clouds when the double-hill landmark of the border showed clearly ahead of them, Coyote Springs laying tucked up against the east flank of the farthest mountain. The pounding of the hoofbeats grew in a crescendo behind them and with the knowledge burning within him that they could be running their horses to death, Hawke asked for all they had to give. With a powerful rhythm they surged forward, rocks and cactus whipping past to either side in a blur. Ahead, Coyote Springs beckoned. Behind, gunshots cracked, echoing hollowly on the morning air.

Hawke glanced over his shoulder. Strung out behind was a knot of three riders, aglow in the light of the early dawn, and less than the length of a passenger train behind came Ramon Ortega and his men. It was hard to tell who was shooting at whom, and Hawke did not look back again. All that was waiting for them lay ahead. Hawke made sure Erin kept to the lead, he and his men ringed out behind her, protecting her back. Jackson rode with his rifle in one hand, as did Pronto. Ringo had his six-gun out, and Rawlins, when Hawke chanced to glance his way, held something that appeared ominous by its very common appearance—a bottle, filled with liquid, and stoppered by a wad of cloth that extended into the bottle and hung outside. Rawlins grinned that slow, confident grin when he saw Hawke's eyes on him and kept riding, holding the bottle wide to one side, the cloth whipping the wind like a flag.

Erin's horse, carrying the lightest burden, was pulling ahead, but as yet she was unaware of it. Hawke hoped to keep it that way. He watched her move with the animal as if she had been born to its back. Describing the wide arch that cut around some foothills, she opened up into the straightaway to Coyote Springs.

Then, out of the corner of his eye, Hawke spotted something else. A couple of horses had separated themselves from the pack Ortega commanded and were cutting through the low hills, closing the gap between them and Erin with gut-wrenching speed. The animal, the one in the lead rode, plunged ahead like a runaway locomotive. As the border approached, the three detectives in the middle were no more than a nuisance between Ortega and his real goal: Erin Keller.

Hawke swore and watched helplessly. They were close, so close. Up ahead a smudged figure of a man appeared on the dun-colored hillside, followed by another and another.

Guns cracked up ahead in warning, and part of the force bringing up the far rear veered off, but the plunging animal pushed on, reaching out for Erin in a dead run. Hawke swore again as he realized she had spotted the lone rider bearing down on her. Altering course, she attempted to move away from him, at the same time forcing her mount into a longer path to Coyote Springs.

Hawke asked his horse for more, wishing his hand rested on the throttle of one of the Indians and he could feel the old familiar burst of speed as the machine surged forward beneath him, not straining every fiber of its being to carry him along.

More shots rang out. Hunched low over his horse's back, face nearly lost in its mane, Hawke was moving with the pounding rhythm when the horse beneath him cut loose with a burst of speed that rocked him in the saddle. Erin was being forced even farther off course. She could have made Coyote Springs and safety if she had just kept on. Even with the rocketing speed it possessed, the big horse would not have been able to catch her in time. But irrational fear did a lot to people, and Hawke knew there could be only one she would be that afraid of now. It had to be Ortega.

Then George Rawlins lit a match, cupped behind the broad break of hand, and touched it to the cloth that dangled from the bottle of liquid. When the flame caught, it burned brightly, unnaturally so, and Rawlins carried it for a few moments like a torch overhead, then casually lobbed it over one shoulder.

Hawke was leaning over his horse's shoulder, aware only of the two riders ahead and the single rider, who appeared from between the hills, pounding in their direction on an intercepting course when the desert to the rear shuddered with the concussion of Rawlins' home-made bomb, which erupted into a wall of flame. Horses panicked, all of them, a few being thrown to their knees by the force of the explosion. Hawke felt his mount do a fast-shuffle sidestep, saw Erin's miss its stride and go down. The rider on the big horse ahead pulled up instantly, grabbed a dazed Erin by the arm, and was trying to hustle her back to his horse as Hawke bore down on them.

His horse barely edged back off full flight, Hawke launched himself from the saddle, the impact taking both Ortega and Erin to the ground with him in a tangle. Ortega turned on him like a wildcat, relinquishing his hold on Erin to transfer it to Hawke.

They tumbled across the hard earth, each locked in the other's death grip, neither landing a blow nor able to disengage a hand to try. With considerable effort, Erin extricated herself from the human heap and staggered to her feet, looking for a way to help.

Seemingly from very far away hoofbeats sounded as Hawke, his head still ringing from the jolt it received when Ortega slammed it against the ground, rolled on top of him. Using his entire body as a battering ram, Hawke slammed against Ortega with all the force he possessed in his well-muscled frame.

Hoofbeats stopped and footsteps sounded as Hawke spotted a rock within reach. With a supreme effort he shifted his grip, felt Ortega go for the opening he presented, then rolled with him again, catching Ortega off balance and rolling him with stunning force against the rock. The bandit grunted and lay still.

Exhausted, Hawke raised his eyes to see a pair of legs with the look of twin tree trunks blocking his view of Erin a few feet beyond. The shadow of a man giant fell across Hawke, blocking the warming sun, and a large hand reached down to lay hold of Ortega's collar, dragging him half-conscious to his feet.

"Thought you could use a hand," Marshal Cook said evenly, "seeing as how you're on American soil anyway."

Bleary-eyed, Hawke looked around him. He did not even want to ask how the hell Cook could tell whether or not they were still in Mexico or across the border.

CHAPTER 18

The water at Coyote Springs was not cool or even very clear, but it was wet and drinkable. Marshal Cook had not brought along the 5th Cavalry, but half an army of work-toughened railroad men were the next best things he could have brought to escort Erin. Her father was there to personally hand over the amnesty papers signed by the governor of the territory above the loud protests made by Tom Fisher. Salvador Hawke figured they were finally coming out on top.

The column of railroad men headed by Cook and Erin's father flanking Ramon Ortega, where he sat mounted on his speedy horse, hands tied behind his back, were ready to pull out almost before all of Hawke's men got to Coyote Springs.

Erin Keller pressed a lingering kiss to Hawke's lips and smiled up into his face. "When will I see you again? How will I find you?" she asked breathlessly, her voice the familiar purr Hawke had first heard back in Ramon Ortega's fortress.

"Don't worry," Hawke told her, "I'll find you," and he was somewhat surprised at himself to realize he meant it.

As the loose column of men pulled out, Maxwell Keller leading off at a brisk gallop, Hawke fingered the fat envelope the man had handed him along with his amnesty papers. Something made him open it and peer inside while Liam Cook sat his horse nearby, waiting, a sardonic grin twisting the corners of his lips.

Hawke muttered an oath and strode purposefully for his horse as Hart Jackson, Pronto, Rawlins, and Ringo gazed after him in puzzlement. The envelope was stuffed with cut-up newspapers and five new one-hundred-dollar bills.

"That was the original bargain," Cook reminded him, bring-

ing Hawke up short. "I wouldn't press my luck if I were you."
The marshal's hand rested casually on the butt of his six-gun.

Without another word Cook wheeled his horse and galloped
after the others. Rawlins strolled over and glanced into the
opened envelope in Hawke's hand, shaking his head when he
saw what lay within.

"Can't trust nobody, not even the law," he lamented, gazing
after the departed marshal.

"I kinda miss them machines, ya know?" Ringo mused.
"Reckon I want to try them things again."

"Takes money," Hawke rejoined, "and we gave our word we
wouldn't be robbing any more trains." He handed each man a
hundred-dollar bill, throwing the cut-up papers in the dirt.
"We're going to keep our word even if those lowlifes didn't."

"Hell, we didn't promise not to rob no banks, did we?" Jackson asked.

"I don't have anything against banks," Hawke observed.

"Ain't got nothing for 'em either, though," Pronto reminded
him, eagerly warming up to Jackson's suggestion.

"True," Hawke admitted.

"Damn right that's true," Ringo enthused, climbing into the
saddle. "What's a bank ever done for us anyhow?"

Hawke sighed and thought of Erin. "We'll have to talk about
it." He swung into the saddle, reined his horse around to the
north, and gave him his head, his men lining out behind him.